STRANGE TIMES
AT FAIRWOOD HIGH

Homeroom

Strange Times at Fairwood High
The Princess of Fairwood High
Triple Trouble at Fairwood High

SCHOLASTIC INC.
New York Toronto London Auckland Sydney

Homeroom

#1

STRANGE TIMES
AT FAIRWOOD HIGH

Nancy Norton

SCHOLASTIC INC.
New York Toronto London Auckland Sydney

ISBN 0-590-41919-6

Copyright © 1988 by Carol Anshaw. All rights reserved. Published by Scholastic Inc. HOMEROOM is a trademark of Scholastic Inc. POINT is a registered trademark of Scholastic Inc.

12 11 10 9 8 7 6 5 4 3 2 1   8 9/8 0 1 2 3/9

Printed in the U.S.A.   01

First Scholastic printing, September 1988

Chapter 1

Piper stood in her new ice-washed jeans, pale blue short-sleeved cotton sweater, and pink high-top sneakers, and clutched her new three-ring notebook across her chest. When she'd left her house that morning, she'd felt totally prepared for the first day of high school. But now, standing in front of Fairwood High, she felt totally *unprepared*.

It seemed like she'd waited years to be there. High school. The Big Time. But now that she finally was there, she suddenly longed to be back at safe little old Crosby Junior High. Where she'd been a big cheese, one of the most popular girls in the ninth grade. Here, she wasn't even a *slice* of cheese. She hardly knew anyone except a few kids from Crosby, and was on the lowest rung of the social ladder — an incoming tenth-grader.

She stood and watched the rush of students hurrying across the lawn, up the walk, through the front doors, hurrying to make the first bell. Piper sighed and ran her free hand through her long blonde hair, and squared her shoulders, getting up the nerve to go on in. Before she could take a step, though, she was suddenly bumped from behind.

"Oh. Sorry," said a cute — very cute — guy with sparkly brown eyes, hair a little spiky in front, and a great smile. He was running backwards across the lawn, and bumped into a couple more kids before leaping up and snapping a red Frisbee out of the air. And then, when he had it, and had dropped back to earth, he turned to Piper and smiled this terrific smile. And then he was off again, up the walk and into the school.

Piper's spirits lifted. She'd only been there two minutes and already a really cute guy had smiled at her. Maybe high school was going to be okay after all.

The first floor hallways were jammed with kids picking up their class schedules for the term. Piper made her way through the crowd, over to the D-E-F table, where she told the girl in charge her name, last name first.

"Davids," she said. "Piper."

She was handed a computer printout sheet, and scanned it. There were all the classes she'd signed up for. She'd have French first thing in the morning. Then geometry, then history. She had first lunch period — 11:30. Good. She couldn't stand the idea of a big breakfast, so she was always starving way before noon.

She read down the list and everything was fine until the very bottom line, which the computer had spit out as:

HOMEROOM: !@#$%^&*

"Darn!" Piper muttered as she found her way to the line in front of the table marked "Problems." Apparently there were a lot of problems. The line stretched down the hall for about twenty kids. Piper looked over the shoulder of the girl standing in front of her. She had the same error on her printout. She turned around and peeked at the sheet in the hand of the guy behind her. Same thing.

"I think we're in the same boat," she said to them. "No homeroom."

"Same here," another guy said, overhearing. He held up his schedule.

Pretty soon, all the kids were gathered around, looking at each others' printouts.

"So?" somebody said. "Who needs a homeroom anyway?" Piper looked up. It was the really cute guy from outside.

"Homeroom is an important part of the school day," said the girl in front of Piper, a tall, thin girl with a confident manner.

She was dressed up in a matching skirt and sweater, and heeled sandals — a more sophisticated look than you usually saw around casual Fairwood, California. "It's where announcements are made, tickets sold, collections taken up, elections held."

"Please excuse me," said a soft voice behind Piper. She turned to see a girl like none she'd ever seen in Fairwood. Tall with shiny jet-black hair. Eyes that were deeper than blue, violet almost. She spoke with an accent that was hard to pin down. Not quite French. Not quite Spanish.

"Yes?" said Piper, curious.

"Just what is this *homeroom*?"

Piper laughed and said, "Are you from this planet?"

She only meant to tease, but the girl looked rattled.

"I . . . I am from Capria."

"Uh?" Piper said, trying to think where Capria was. "Oh, yeah. That's down around San Diego, isn't it?"

"No. It is a country. It is in Europe."

"Oh, yeah — Europe," Piper said, trying to sound casual, as if she went there every other day and knew it like the back of her hand. Actually, she'd never been farther than Disneyland, and was a little embarrassed by this fact. "So you're like an exchange student here?" she asked the girl.

4

"Something like exchanging, yes," the girl said and smiled a little nervously. "My name is Tamara." She held out her hand, but not as if to shake Piper's. She held it palm down, like the Pope does when offering his ring to be kissed. It was pretty odd, but Piper figured this was the way they did it in Capria. Not knowing what to do, she took Tamara's hand and commented on her nails.

"Nice shade of polish."

"Ah, many thanks," Tamara replied, then added with pride. "I applied it all by myself."

Well, rooty-toot-toot for you, Piper thought, but didn't say anything. Maybe in Capria, everyone painted each other's nails.

"Boys and girls!" A woman was shouting over the noise in the hallway. "I'm Ms. Gilley, the assistant principal. As you've probably gathered, we've had a computer foul-up this morning and all of you . . ." she gestured to include everyone standing in the group in front of the "Problems" table, ". . . all of you should have been assigned to your alphabetical homerooms, but alas, here you are." She sighed and looked at them as if *they* were creating the problem.

"We'll just have to lump you all together into a new homeroom. The only problem is that we don't really have one, *or* a home-room teacher for you. The best we can do is put you in 434 down at the far end of the old 400 wing," she said, pointing off in the distance. "We've been using it for storage these past few years, so it may be a little dusty. But if you'll all go down there and make yourselves as comfortable, and as *quiet*, as possible, we'll try to round up a teacher for you as soon as possible."

Piper turned to Tamara. She wanted to make up for teasing her before. "Come on. We can walk together."

"May I escort you, ladies?" The really cute guy had come up to them and was making a little bow, like a character out of an old English play. Piper giggled, but Tamara took the gesture absolutely seriously and held out her hand again. Without missing a beat, the really cute guy bent from the waist and kissed the back of it, then stood up and grinned again.

"I am Prin . . . I am Tamara," the foreign girl introduced herself.

"Hi," he said. "Judd Peterson." He turned to Piper with a question mark in his eyes.

"Piper," she said, as they started walking along together. "Piper Davids. Tamara's an exchange student. Maybe you can help me explain to her what homeroom is."

Judd laughed. "Well, it's kind of this

rushed little stretch of time first thing in the morning when they try to get you all confused about everything that's happening in school before the day even begins. Actually, homeroom is usually the most boring part of the day."

Not *this* homeroom, Piper thought, looking at him while trying hard not to look like she was.

Chapter 2

"What is this?! The Temple . . ." said the first person to enter room 434.

". . . of Doom!" said the next. Piper looked up. There were only two people she knew who finished each others' sentences — Casey and Cathy Connor, the two people she'd most hoped she'd left behind in junior high. Back at Crosby, they'd been known as "Double Trouble," always up to no good. Although they weren't very smart at anything else, the twins were positive geniuses at stirring up confusion and conspiracy, schemes and plots — sometimes to get what they wanted, sometimes just to be mean. And here they were, smack-dab in Piper's homeroom where she'd have to deal with them every day until next June.

For the moment, she pretended she didn't see them, staying instead with Judd and Tamara, looking around the room. It was a pretty grim sight. Clearly 434 hadn't been used as a classroom in some time. The walls were scuffed up, the windows filmed over with grime. The desks were wooden ones so old they had inkwell holes. The bulletin board was decorated with bleached-out construction-paper turkeys and Pilgrims, and essays on Thanksgiving penned in faded ink on loose-leaf sheets yellowed with age.

The back wall was lined with metal shelves stacked with sports equipment. A couple of guys had already pulled on football helmets and tattered shoulder pads and were flipping an imaginary ball back and forth.

"American boys?" Tamara said to Piper. "They are a little silly?"

Piper turned to Judd and passed the question along. "Well?"

"Well, I can't speak for all American guys," he said in mock seriousness, "but I myself am *never, ever* silly."

"Oh, *right*, Superboy," said one of the other guys in a tone dripping with sarcasm. He was tall and blond with thin, horn-rimmed glasses. He was wearing a blue oxford cloth shirt, and beat-up khakis with red suspenders. Mr. Junior Corporate, Piper thought as he introduced himself.

"T. Craig Yarmouth," he said. "Remember the name. I may be your class president."

"Not so fast," said the sophisticated girl who'd given the little lecture on homerooms. "I plan to run for that office myself. Tiffany Taylor is *my* name. You'll probably be seeing a lot of it on posters and such when I get my campaign going."

Class president? Piper thought. We haven't even been in school an hour and these two are already on the campaign trail! She was relieved when both of them went on to shake other hands, meet other voters. Her own mind couldn't have been further away from politics. She had a question to ask Judd.

"Just what did he mean, calling you Superboy?"

"Oh," Judd said, running a hand through the spiky front of his hair. "Last Halloween, I climbed up the Fairwood water tower in a Superboy outfit."

"I thought you looked a little familiar," she said. She'd been trying to place his face ever since she'd first seen him that morning.

"Yeah," he said shyly. "It kind of made the papers."

"Why'd you do it?" Piper asked.

"I don't know. To see if I could."

"Excuse me," said Tamara, who was clearly lost, "but who is this Superboy?"

"It looks like we're going to have to give you a crash course in American pop culture, Tammy," Judd said, and immediately a large hand slammed onto his shoulder with an iron grip.

"Her name is Tamara," said a deep, menacing voice. They all turned to see who it belonged to. He was a hulking guy, at least eighteen years old, wearing a suit, which *no one* ever did around Fairwood High. He looked completely out of place. He turned to Tamara and said in a stern tone, "What is going on here? I turn my back at the registration and you are gone." He looked around the storeroom. "And what is this?"

"It is a mistake, Adolfo," Tamara said nervously. "They are correcting it. There is no problem. Please. You must leave." He looked at her for a moment longer, then nodded, and left. Tamara stood watching him go and then turned back to her new friends, trying to think of some way to explain.

"He is my . . . my brother."

"A little overprotective, wouldn't you say?" Judd said, rubbing his shoulder where Adolfo had clamped it. "Just a minor fracture. Nothing to worry about."

"I am so sorry. It is just that he worries about me. I will talk with him tonight at . . . at home. It will not happen again." The way she said this struck Piper as odd. It wasn't as though she was going to have a brother-sister chat with Adolfo, more like she was going to *command* him not to interfere. There was something about Tamara that wasn't like other girls, probably not like other girls in Capria, either, she bet.

"Uh, excuse me," said a husky girl's voice that came with a tap on Piper's shoulder. "Could you keep standing right there so I can hide behind you?"

Piper started to turn around.

"No! Don't! He'll see!" whispered the girl frantically.

Piper looked to see who "he" might be. Most of the guys were preoccupied with the imaginary football game. The girl with the husky voice had to be referring to the retro-looking guy in the ducktail haircut and leather jacket who'd just come through the door, and was scanning the scene. When he had spotted a friend among the football players and had gone over, Piper figured it was safe to see just who it was she was hiding. She turned to find a pretty girl with short, frizzed blonde hair. Very chic in tweed baggies, a T-shirt and a thrift shop men's sports jacket. She didn't look like someone who'd be hiding from anyone. And she really didn't look like someone who'd be connected with a guy as tough-looking as the one who'd just come into the room. Piper gave the girl a question-mark look to see if she wanted to talk about it.

"Ancient history," the girl said, then laughed and introduced herself. "I'm Karen Murchinson. Eddie and I used to go out together. I thought I was leaving him and *everything* about junior high behind. I *thought* I was going to Chopin. You know, the fine arts high school. I'm an *actress*. But my folks wouldn't let me go to Chopin, so here I am. And here *he* is. The *irony* of it, if you know what I mean. I was hoping I wouldn't run into him until we could both be comfortable talking to each other. You know, like about *thirty years* from now." Karen spoke dramatically, emphasizing every few words — it was the way she thought an actress should talk.

"But you can't hide forever. You're going to see him in here every day," Piper said.

The girl nodded. "I *know*. You're *right*. I've got to be *mature* about this. But for now, could you just keep standing right there?"

By now, things had gone from pretty rowdy to total pandemonium in room 434. The guys had found a real football and brought the scrimmage out of the realm of the imaginary into hard-hitting reality.

The twins had turned on their mini-boom box and were dancing. Tiffany was standing at the front of the room, trying to call everyone to order, but no one was paying a bit of attention to her.

Suddenly into the middle of this came a piercing screech. Everyone stopped where they were and looked toward the door. There, almost filling the doorway, was an extremely tall, extremely well-muscled, extremely handsome guy with a blond crew-cut.

"*This* is more how I imagined American boys," Tamara whispered to Piper.

"Then you have quite an imagination. Hardly any of them look like this. And this is not a boy, this is a *man*."

Having frozen everyone with the blast from his whistle, the man in the doorway stood silent himself for a moment. When he spoke, it was in a surprisingly soft voice, tinged with shyness.

"Uh, I'm Ted Talbot. I coach the basketball and football teams here at Fairwood. I'm . . . uh . . . I'm not used . . . well, actually, I've never done any homeroom duty. I'm about as new to this as you are. We'll just have to figure it out together." He looked around at 434, and said dryly, "Well, at least they gave us the best room in the house."

From total silence, the room exploded

into laughter. Everyone knew in that instant that whatever else high school held in store for them, homeroom was going to be *different*.

"Now you'd all better get out of here," Coach Talbot said. "You're five minutes late for first period as it is. I'll try to get maintenance to clean this place up tonight, but maybe you could all bring something — anything — tomorrow to spruce the place up a little."

Piper said a quick good-bye to Tamara and dashed. She didn't want to make a bad impression on the French teacher right off the bat. She was a ways down the hall when she felt a presence running beside her. It was Judd.

"Hey. Want to go see the new Woody Allen picture with me Friday night?"

She was stunned. She had hoped he had really noticed her, but she hadn't expected anything to happen so soon. She hadn't even been to her first class in high school and she already had her first date. Or would, if she could make her mouth say the word.

"Yes," she finally blurted out and they both laughed, and then smiled at each other. For no reason at all.

Chapter 3

Tamara's first day at Fairwood High rushed by in a blur of confusing impressions. *Everything* there was so different from her life back home. Of course "home" was very far away, in a tiny mountain kingdom. And her life in Capria was an ivory tower existence, sheltered from the rough and tumble of ordinary life. She was tired of this, and had been ecstatic when her parents told her they were sending her to America. Finally she'd get a chance at what every other teenage girl took for granted — a regular, maybe even sometimes boring, life, but with dating and friends and adventure.

But now that she was actually there in California, enrolled at Fairwood High, she wasn't sure it had been such a great idea. With her textbook English, she understood most of what was going on in her classes, but outside them she could barely make out a word anyone was saying. What did "catch you later" mean? And what was a "party animal"? Why did boys hit each other, then laugh? Why were the girls always whispering with each other? And what were "Sloppy Joes"? She felt hopelessly shut out, worse even than at home. Here, everyone probably thought she was foreign, or stupid.

And so she was in a pit of depression when she rounded the corner toward home. Adolfo silently fell into step beside her.

"Talk to me," she said to him. "You must try to seem like my brother. Ask me how my day at school went."

He nodded. "How did your day at school went?" His English was not as good as Tamara's.

"Not so well. There is too much I don't understand."

"It is only your first day. And the customs here are strange indeed. I have been watching and listening."

"Oh? And what are your observations?"

"The girls are pretty, but all they talk about is each other, and their boyfriends, and some people they all seem to know who live in a place called Knots Landing."

"And the boys?" Tamara asked.

"They hit each other to show their friendship."

"Yes, I, too, have noticed this."

"And they don't play frescuball. And none of them seems to know anything about farming or livestock."

"Hmmm," Tamara said, taking all this in.

"And the main place of meeting for all these young people seems to be some place called 'the mall.' "

"Mall?"

"Yes, I am sure I have heard this correctly."

"Try to find out what this 'mall' is. I am curious."

"I will do my best," Adolfo promised.

"And try not to be so rough. You practically injured that poor boy in my homeroom." Tamara looked at him disapprovingly.

"My apologies. I will try to be more discreet."

When they had walked to the edge of town, they arrived at the hacienda-style house her parents had rented for her.

"Hello, Tomás," she said to the butler as she came in.

"Did you find school a satisfactory experience?" he asked politely.

"Oh, the school part is all right. It is the . . . the *un*-school part that is sad-making," Tamara said dejectedly. "One girl was friendly, but then she immediately found a boyfriend. Everyone pairs off and finds friends, but I am odd and different. I shall find no friends here in Fairwood, I'm afraid."

"You must give these things time. Perhaps you should talk with Maria." Maria was her dear maid from home.

She poked her head out of the kitchen now and asked Tamara, "Would you like me to prepare your tea now?"

"I think in America, teenagers don't have tea in the afternoons," Tamara informed her. "They have snacks." Adolfo nodded in agreement.

"And just what would these snacks be?" Maria said, dubious about the whole proposition.

Adolfo cleared his throat and injected his expert opinion, based on a day's observation.

"As far as I can see, the three main snack foods are large triangles of something dripping cheese, orange puffs called 'doodles', and something that is drunk by a tube out of a large cup. It is, I believe, called a 'Slurpee.' "

"Ah," Maria said. "I see. I will have to inquire at the grocery for these important snack items. I assume they are very nutritious."

Up in her bedroom, which had been furnished for her from pictures of teenage bedrooms in decorator magazines, a lonely Tamara sat in front of her small TV and watched a show set in a hospital. All the doctors and nurses were in love with each other, and sometimes with patients. Tamara found the show quite comic, although she suspected she wasn't supposed to. "Catch you later," one of the characters said to another. And then, in a commercial, a small dog appeared in a sailor suit.

"Ah," she sighed. "At least now I understand who the party animal is."

She had heard someone use the expression in school that day. She got out a leather-covered notebook and began taking down all the expressions she didn't understand. She would make a list and ask Piper, the nice girl in homeroom. Piper who already had a boy interested in her. Tamara sighed again. Would she ever have friends and a boyfriend and "catch someone later" or "see them around"? Although she'd come all the way over oceans and continents to get to Fairwood, now that she was there, she still felt a million miles away from fitting in.

And even if she could find a way to begin fitting in, sooner or later someone was bound to discover her *big* secret — and then they would treat her as the ultimate outsider. Just as they did in Capria.

Chapter 4

The second day of school, Piper walked into room 434 carrying her contribution to the room's decor — an enormous old bowling trophy from her dad's college days in the sixties. The little bronze bowler on top had bell-bottom pants. It was the worst hunk of junk she could find in an hour of looking in the garage.

As she came through the door, she burst out laughing. Apparently everyone in the homeroom had gotten the same idea. It looked like each of them had brought something hideous, worthless, ridiculous, or weird. Karen had brought a painting of a sad clown done on black velvet. Sitting on Eddie's desk was a lamp that gurgled and bubbled. Tiffany was holding a stuffed owl on a fake branch. T. Craig was rolling out a green putting carpet in front of Coach Talbot's desk. Judd was sticking a Nerf ball hoop onto the blackboard. Tamara was the only one who'd taken the coach's request seriously; she'd brought a nice vase filled with roses. She was looking at the other offerings with bewilderment.

"Wow!" Piper exclaimed, coming into this scene. "It looks like a picture from *Better Homes and Asylums*!"

Everyone cracked up at this, and then suddenly hushed into total silence, with all eyes on the door behind Piper. She turned to see Coach Talbot looming behind her, looking around the room, surveying what the kids had done to it. Everyone held their breath waiting for his reaction.

"Perfect!" he shouted. "Just the atmosphere for my own personal contribution." And with this, he unfurled the giant poster he had in his hands. As it rolled open to the floor, everyone saw that it was a bigger-than-life photo of Beaver Cleaver, from the old TV series.

"Right on," Judd shouted, as the twins passed it to T. Craig and Eddie, who stood on chairs to hang it with push pins on the back wall.

"Now, I'm afraid we must get down to the business of morning announcements," Coach Talbot said, pulling a fistful of Xeroxed pages from the pocket of his sweatpants. He was visibly nervous, shifting from one foot to the other. He was used to coaching, to being around sports, and roughhousing guys. It was clear he felt ill at ease in this classroom, and with all these girls, half of them looking at him with dreamy expressions because he was so cute. He cleared his throat and began reading.

"First, those students wishing to take the nutritious hot lunch provided by the school cafeteria — " He was forced to stop because of all the loud groaning coming from the kids who'd tried the hot lunch the day before. " — will have to buy their lunch passes by Friday. Next, there will be a football pep rally Friday after school for all those interested in firing up our Falcons for their first game of the season. . . ."

As the coach read on, Piper found a seat, and then looked over across the room and smiled at Judd. He looked even cuter today in a red sweatshirt, his hair still damp from the shower, his eyes still a little sleepy.

He smiled back at her, then pulled a pen from a shirt pocket, and began scribbling something in his spiral notebook. When he was done he ripped the page out, folded it in half, then in quarters, then again, and again, until it was a small fat square. He handed it to Tamara, indicating that she should pass it on down toward Piper.

When Piper finally got the note, she opened it to read:

> *You look great today. Are you sure you still want to go out with me Friday? You could have any guy in school.*

She took out her pen and wrote in small round script at the bottom:

> *Every one of them called last night, but I turned them all down, so I'm still free. You'll have to meet my parents when you come by. Is that okay?*

When he got the note back and read it, he nodded across the room, and made an "okay" sign with his thumb and finger.

Tamara passed these notes back and forth. She didn't know exactly what they said, but she had a rough idea. Things weren't *completely* different in Capria. She wondered if she would find someone here in Fairwood, the way Piper and Judd were finding each other. So far, none of the boys she'd seen interested her. None except Coach Talbot, who was not a boy. Who was, in fact, a teacher and therefore completely off-limits. Well, she could have her dreams. She sat back and closed her eyes and listened to him reading the announcements.

His voice sounded *so* romantic as he read:

"Student cars must be parked in the student lot only. Student cars found in the teachers' lot. . . ."

In the back of the room, two students sat unable to hear a word the coach was saying. Every ounce of their energy was focused on ignoring each other. Karen and Eddie had wound up sitting side by side, and had to stare straight ahead to avoid any eye contact.

He was still too angry to talk with her. She was too embarrassed to talk to him. Last spring it had seemed so clear that she was leaving him behind, that she was moving onward and upward in life — to Chopin, the fine arts high school, then to New York for acting classes. Then to the stage, movies. But now, thanks to her parents, there she was, neither onward nor upward — just there. Worse than just there, she was there and smack next to Eddie Baker.

After five minutes of staring at the blackboard, Karen gave up. This was just too hard, and too weird. So she put on her most sincere fake smile and turned his way.

"Hey, Eddie," she said in her coolest voice. "How's it going?"

He pulled himself out of his usual slouch

and pushed his sunglasses down onto his nose and looked as if he didn't quite recognize her. The creep. He was going to make this tough on her.

"Oh. Karen. Hi. Yeah, things are going great for me. Not so great for you, I gather. You didn't get into Chopin, I guess."

"Of course I got in," Karen snapped. "It's just that my parents didn't think I'd get a broad enough education there."

"Oh, yeah," he said, making it supremely clear that he wasn't believing a word of this. "Sure."

Karen flushed with anger. She could feel her ears getting hot. She tried with all her might, though, not to let him see that he was getting to her.

"Eddie," she said, edging each word with frost. "Believe whatever you want. I couldn't care less." She glanced out of the corners of her eyes to see his reaction, but he was already sliding his Walkman headphones onto his ears, putting a casually insulting end to the conversation.

She swallowed hard to fight back tears of humiliation. She was not about to let him see he had any effect on her at all. If she was half the actress she thought she was, she should be able to pull this off.

"Oh, Coach," she shouted out lightly, raising her hand. "Where is it you said we should pick up our lunch passes?" It was the first thing she could think of to say. Instantly she regretted it. Now she would have to actually take the dreaded hot lunch. Even in junior high, they'd heard about it. Fish with heads and eyes. Mystery meat. Rainbow lunch meat. The rumors were endless. Karen gulped and smiled bravely.

Out in the hall, the bell rang for change of classes. At the doorway, Tamara caught up with Piper.

"Maybe I could ask you some questions?" she said, holding open a small leather notebook. "About how things are done here, about what everything means. I am confused."

Piper smiled and draped an arm across Tamara's shoulders and looked down into the notebook.

"Sure. Let's see what you've got here. *Gross me out!* You want to know what that means?"

"Please," Tamara said.

"Well, it means something sickening. Like, if someone barfs."

"Barfs?" Tamara said.

"Throws up," Piper said, giving a little visual demonstration.

"Oh, my," said Tamara, who wasn't used to discussing such things.

"But most of the time you use it sarcastically — you know. Someone wears a really ugly sweater and you say to someone else, 'Gross me out,' like it's so bad it's going to make you sick."

"I see," Tamara said. "In my country it is very different. We would just say, 'Your sweater is extremely ugly.'"

"Right to the person's face?" Piper asked.

"We are very honest in Capria."

"Well, I wouldn't advise *that* much honesty around here. You might get clobbered."

"What is this *clobbered*?" Tamara asked.

Piper laughed. "Better put it on your list. This is my French class," she nodded toward the classroom they were standing in front of. "Looks like you're going to have a lot of questions, for a while anyway. Why don't we meet after school and go for a Coke and fries or something and I'll try to answer them."

Tamara nodded, and added "fries" to the list.

"You are nice to me," she told Piper.

"It's easy." This was true. Even though Tamara was the most unusual girl Piper had ever met, there was something likable about her. Plus, Piper felt a little protective. She suspected Tamara was going to have a bit of a rough time at Fairwood, where there were a lot of tight cliques and the kids who were different were usually shut out.

As she waved good-bye to Tamara and turned into her French class, Piper glimpsed the twins, Cathy and Casey, watching Tamara and whispering to each other. Always gossiping, she thought, then stopped inside the door to wonder — gossiping about *what*?

Chapter 5

Casey and Cathy sat under a tree on the campus lawn after school. They were sharing a bag of chips, in spite of their promise to each other to start their diet that week. The twins were always either on a new diet, or planning to start one, or falling off one. In spite of this, they were both always about ten pounds overweight. When one gained a pound, so did the other. When one lost, they both did. It was uncanny. A lot of things about them were a little uncanny.

"He's the cutest guy . . ." Casey was saying.

". . . in the whole school," Cathy finished the sentence for her. "I know you think that, but what about Steve Feder?"

"Steve looks too much like a movie star. Plus he knows how good-looking he is. Which kind of ruins it. I mean, you know how he's always running his hand through his hair? Judd never does anything like that. And think of the luck, getting put in the same homeroom with him. It's almost like . . . fate, don't you think?"

"Yeah," Cathy agreed. "But I think you're too late."

"What do you mean — too late?!" Casey said in an amazed voice.

"Well . . ." her sister said, drawing out the suspense, ". . . according to what *I've* heard, he likes Piper Davids. They've got a date this weekend."

"Piper? Well, it's only one date," Casey said smugly.

"Yeah, I don't think they're getting married or anything yet," Cathy said sarcastically.

"Then there's still time," Casey mused. "But we'll have to move *fast*."

"Speak of the devil," Cathy nudged her twin as Piper walked past them.

"And look who's with her," Casey said. "E.T. The extraterrestrial."

"I told you Casey, that Tamara's a spy. I mean, did you even hear of that country she's supposed to be from? And that brother? That suit of his? Give me a break. I say she's got a *big* secret. I'm sure she's a spy. She's probably KGB."

"Let's follow them," Casey said, getting up, crumpling the chip bag, and tossing it behind the tree. "We can hear what Piper has to say about her date with Judd."

"And what that Tamara gives away about herself. *Nobody* gets to keep secrets from The Twins."

Following people was one of the twins' favorite occupations, coming not too far after eavesdropping and spreading rumors. They had never been able to make friends and so they had started acting hostilely to everyone. That had caused the kids to exclude the twins further, and so the vicious circle had begun. Now the twins were too caught up in their sly maneuvers to change.

"Let's go to The Thermos, okay?" Piper said to Tamara when they were off campus, walking toward the center of Fairwood.

"Oh, fine," Tamara said, not having the vaguest idea what The Thermos was.

Piper saw this, and said, "It's an old coffee shop from the fifties. The kids around here have pretty much taken it over. A real teen hangout."

"Hangout?" Tamara said.

"A . . . a meeting place," Piper said by way of explanation.

"Ah . . . like the mall," Tamara said brightly.

"No," Piper laughed. "Not like the mall. Come on. You'll see."

They got there just in time. The Thermos was already beginning to fill up with the after-school crowd, but Piper found an empty booth in the back.

"What is this machine?" Tamara said, immediately drawn to the old mini-jukebox hanging on the wall in the booth.

"You put a quarter in here," Piper said, "and it plays your favorite song."

"Oh, I doubt that," Tamara said and laughed. "My favorite song is 'The Happy Glockenspiel.'"

"It sounds like rock and roll hasn't hit Capria yet," Piper said. "Well, it'll be interesting to see what you make of American music. Here's a start." She slapped a quarter down on the formica tabletop, and the two of them began flipping through the possible selections.

This distracted them enough so that they didn't notice the twins slide by and into the booth behind theirs.

"I think I will choose this one. By David Bowie," Tamara at last decided, and dropped in the quarter. "And now . . ." she said eagerly, "some nutritious American snack foods."

Piper burst out laughing, and said, "Oh, yes, incredibly nutritious." Then she said to the waitress who had come up to the booth, "Two Tabs and an order of cheese fries!"

"Oh, cheese fries sound so good," Casey whispered to Cathy in the next booth. "Do you think we can have an order? I mean, we did already have that bag of chips."

"Oh, I think it'll be okay. After all, cheese is healthy. And both things are potatoes. You're supposed to have plenty of vegetables on this diet."

"Shhh," Casey said. "I think they're talking about You-Know-Who now."

"So you will be marrying him?" Tamara was asking innocently.

"Marry?" Piper said in amazement. "We haven't even had our first *date* yet."

"Then this is not being arranged by your parents? Many marriages in Capria, even among commoners, are arranged by the parents. The bride brings a dowry of goats, or pastureland."

"Sounds real romantic," Piper teased.

"Oh, you are *romantic* about Judd?" Tamara said, which embarrassed Piper a little. She wasn't used to such direct questions.

"Well, I like him. I think he likes me. Wait until after Friday and I'll tell you more. And thanks for passing our notes. It helps to have a postman."

"You will especially tell the postman if there is kissing?" Tamara asked. "I am very interested in kissing, which I have not done yet, only read about."

"You've never kissed *anybody?*" Piper said.

Tamara shook her head, her long dark hair tossing around her shoulders.

"I lead a very . . . protected life in my country," Tamara said. It sounded to Piper like she was choosing her words carefully, as though she wasn't saying all she wanted to say. Piper looked up and was surprised to see Tamara's brother Adolfo. He was standing across the room, leaning against the wall next to the pay phone, watching them.

"Oh, look, Tamara. There's your brother."

Tamara looked up and over at Adolfo. She nodded and he nodded back. Neither of them smiled, and she didn't invite him over. And he didn't leave, but continued to stand there watching them.

"Where is the servant with the snack foods?" Tamara said now, looking around for the waitress, clearly trying to change the subject.

"Will you look at that!" Cathy whispered to her sister, pointing toward Adolfo. "If that hulking creep's her brother, then *I'm* Madonna."

"Yeah, yeah. They're definitely spies,"

Casey agreed, but she wasn't really interested in Tamara. "Did you hear what Piper said about passing notes with Judd? *That* is interesting!"

"What's so interesting?" Cathy asked.

Casey ran a comb through her short dark hair and adjusted the bright red bracelet on her wrist. "If one person can write a note, another person can write a note, and if the handwriting looks alike who will know who wrote what note?"

Cathy just stared. "I don't get you."

Casey huffed impatiently. "Sometimes, I don't believe you are *my* twin. You can be *so* thick. What I mean is, I could write a note to Judd that he will think is from Piper and really mess things up."

"Ohhh," Cathy breathed.

"Ohhh," Casey mimicked.

Chapter 6

"Is there more taco stuff?" Piper's father asked.

"Mmmhmmm," Piper muttered through a mouthful of refried beans, and got up from the table.

"Me, too," her younger sister Molly said, holding out her plate to Piper.

On Friday afternoons, Piper's mother had teachers' meetings at her school, and so Piper cooked dinner for the family. Which meant they got either tacos, or tuna casserole, or grilled cheese sandwiches, the three things she knew how to fix. Tacos were her best shot. She just made the filling from ground beef and a package of mix, but she always made sure to set out all the toppings — sour cream, shredded cheese, black olives, and avocado slices. The "taco bar," she called it. Sometimes she thought that if nothing else in life worked out for her, she could always open a stand

and make a million dollars with her truly superb tacos.

Tonight, though, she'd forgotten both the black olives and the avocados. A first. It was because her mind was completely elsewhere. The honest truth was that she'd only had about three dates in her entire life, and they'd all been with boys she hadn't cared anything about . . . until tonight. Tonight, in exactly one hour and seventeen minutes, Judd Peterson was going to be standing at the front door, ringing the bell. Piper's mind simply was not on tacos.

Still, she managed to put seconds on everyone's plate, sit back down at her place, and get a reasonably cool expression on her face. Or so she thought.

"Why do you look like you're about to have a heart attack?" her mother asked.

"Uh, well, I guess I'm a little nervous. I've . . . uh . . . got this kind of . . . well . . . date tonight."

"Date?" her father said. "With whom?" In spite of having been a laid-back hippie in the sixties, her father was kind of a strict dad. If she went out, he and her mom had to know where, and with whom, and when she was coming back. And they checked sometimes, so she couldn't lie like some of her friends did. In a way this was kind of a drag, and in another way it was kind of a security blanket.

"Judd," Piper said.

"Judd who?" her mother asked.

"Peterson. He's great. You'll like him."

"*We'll* be the judge of that," her dad said, crossing his arms across his chest, pretending to look severe. "Does he follow the Dodgers? Does he like to help older guys paint their garages?" (This was his project for the weekend.) "Does he believe in rock and roll?"

Piper's dad was an oldies freak. Even now, as he got up and went over to the sink to rinse the dishes, he was holding a dish with one hand, and flipping on the radio.

"*Yes, I heard it through the grapevine, and I'm just about to lo-ose my mind . . .*" he sang along with Marvin Gaye. He would sing along with any song he knew, although he thought he was best as Paul McCartney or a Supreme. The worst and most embarrassing part of this was what a terrible voice he had. As Piper's mother put it (when he wasn't around), he couldn't carry a tune in a bucket.

"Uh, Dad," Piper said now, bringing her empty plate over to the sink, "maybe you could not sing for just a little while — like, say, the little while that Judd's here?"

"Oh, no!" he said, clutching his chest

and doubling over, pretending to be wounded. "The critics are out to get me! They want to silence the great Carlos!" His name was really Charles, but he'd made up this joke about himself as Carlos. Piper and her mother and Molly were the Carlettes, his backup group. Sometimes Piper thought her family was pretty funny; sometimes she was totally embarrassed by them. It depended on her mood.

"Please," she said to her father. He turned around and looked at her and said. "Oh, all right. Spoilsport. Wet blanket. We could've put on a real show for the guy. But okay. We'll just sit around the living room and ask him how he likes school. We'll be as normal as a TV family." He turned to Piper's mother and Molly, who were still sitting at the table.

"We'll be incredibly normal," Piper's mother said. "I'll be knitting."

"I'll wear my fatherly sweater and be reading the paper. The dog will sit at my feet."

"We don't have a dog," Piper pointed out.

"Oh, right. Then we'll have to do the best we can without one."

"Can I wear my bat costume?" Molly said. She already had Halloween on the brain.

"Atta girl," Piper's dad said.

"Hadn't you better get ready?" Mrs. Davids asked Piper. "Aren't teenage girls supposed to spend about four hours getting ready for a date?"

"Oh, right," Piper said, although she couldn't think of anything much to do to get ready. And so she just sat up in her room, and played a few records, and put on some fresh blusher, and ran a brush through her hair, and put on the outfit she'd already decided to wear — a black skirt and sweater. Being blonde, she thought black was her best color. It was a matter of contrast.

When she was ready, there were still forty-two minutes left. So she just sat down in the old overstuffed chair in the corner of her room and thought how great everything was going. Her homeroom was wild. She'd made a new friend in Tamara. And of course, there was Judd. In spite of telling Tamara she didn't know what was going to happen between them, secretly she hoped this was going to be a wonderful romance. And she just knew tonight was going to be the best date of her life, even if there had only been three. Her parents were in a great mood. Judd was going to like them and they were going to *love* him. She held her breath for a moment, to savor the feeling of pure perfection.

And the moment held, for a while anyway. Her family behaved normally — well, almost. And they liked Judd.

He arrived ten minutes early, before anyone was expecting him. Piper was upstairs, pretending to be taking forever to get ready, to satisfy her mother's notion of what a regular teenage girl should do before a date. Actually she was going through her closet, looking at her clothes to see if she could recombine them so that it would look like she had more outfits than she really did.

She babysat regularly Tuesday and Saturday nights for the kids down the block ("The Hendersons From Horror House"), which gave her some extra spending money, but between all the tapes she wanted, and books, and funky earrings, which she never could resist, there was never enough left over for all the clothes that caught her eye out at the mall that her mother didn't want to give her money for.

When the bell rang, she was in the middle of going through a drawer full of her oldest sweaters — some that went back to eighth grade. She jumped up and opened the bedroom door so she could hear what was going on downstairs.

The rest of her famliy — that is, Carlos and two of the Carlettes — were down in the living room, doing a big lip-sync and pantomime production of "You Can't Hurry Love" when the bell rang. Piper held her breath, but then, mercifully, the stereo volume went way down and she heard her father answering the door like a regular person, welcoming Judd inside. Piper smoothed down her sweater, gave herself a quick look in the mirror, and rushed down the stairs.

She couldn't help but smile when she saw Judd. He'd dressed up for the date. That is, he was not only wearing jeans and a T-shirt, but also a linen sports jacket. She could tell he was a little nervous in this "Meeting-the-Parents" situation. He was wringing his hands and smiling in a strained way.

When her dad asked him, "Do you enjoy painting garages?" Judd replied, without missing a beat, "Funny you should mention that. I'm almost a jinx at garages. People have actually paid me to *not* paint theirs."

Piper saw her dad laughing at this as she came down the stairs. Everything was going to be all right between the two of them. Her mother, though, was acting a little weird.

"Peterson, Peterson," she kept muttering to herself. "Where do I know you from?" Then she turned to Judd and asked, "Do you by chance have any kid sisters or brothers who go to Kammer grade school?

I teach there, and your name is so familiar."

Judd shook his head. "Nope, I'm afraid I'm an only child," he said politely.

"Hmmm," Piper's mother said, driving Piper crazy. Why didn't she just drop this? But instead she just went on. "The odd thing is — you *look* so familiar, too." She snapped her fingers. "I know! You bag groceries over at the supermarket, don't you?"

He shook his head again.

"Oh, well," she said, finally walking them to the door, "it'll come to me. You two have a good time now. What are you going to see?"

"The new Woody Allen," Piper answered.

"I just said that to get her to go out with me," Judd teased. "We're really going to see the new Arnold Schwarzenegger."

"Argh," Piper groaned, as the two of them went out the door.

When they were outside, walking across the front lawn, he put an arm around her shoulders and kissed her cheek quickly. She looked at Judd in surprise. She didn't mind . . . but so fast?

"What's a guy to do?" he said, throwing up his hands. "You just look so great. I had to kiss you right away or it would have been on my mind all night. Now I can concentrate on getting us to the movie. Come on. Hop on behind me," he said, getting onto the red motor scooter parked in the drive.

Piper stopped and stared. She hadn't known he had a scooter, and she'd just assumed they'd be walking to the show. She wondered if the scooter would be okay with her folks.

She didn't have to wonder for long. She'd barely gotten on behind Judd, barely put her arms around his waist, when the front door opened and her dad appeared on the porch.

"Uh, Piper," he said in an odd, formal voice, completely different from how he'd been talking with them five minutes before. "Would you come back in for a minute?"

Piper looked at Judd, answering the unspoken question in his eyes with a shrug. She had no idea what was going on.

When she got inside, both her parents were waiting in the front hall.

"I finally remembered where I've seen him before," her mother said. There was no fun in her voice, either. "The newspaper. He's some kind of daredevil. Climbed the water tower."

"That was just fooling around," Piper

rushed to Judd's defense. "The kids call him Superboy. It's just a joke kind of thing."

"What about the accident he got into? That made the paper, too. Was that also just a joke?" her mother asked.

"What accident?" Piper said.

"Ask him," her mother said cryptically.

"Yes. When you go to tell him you're not going to have this, or any, date with him," her father said.

"What?!" Piper cried.

"You heard your father. We can't let you go out with someone who's so clearly reckless. Dangerous, even," Piper's mother said. "Piper, be sensible."

"We'll leave the scooter here," Piper said in desperation. "We'll just *walk* to the show."

"Sorry," her father said. "It's not his wheels we're worried about. It's his attitude. Piper, the boy has a bad reputation. He's irresponsible."

"But — "

"No buts. I know you're disappointed, but this is for your own good," he said.

"This is what parents are for," her mother said. "Making you a little miserable now so that you don't end up majorly miserable later, spending the rest of your life in traction."

"Give me a break," Piper muttered to

herself as she stalked out of the house, burning with anger and humiliation. How was she going to tell Judd she couldn't go out with him because her parents thought he was a maniac?

"I can't go out with you because my parents think you're a maniac," she said, deciding on the unvarnished truth.

"Ah," Judd said, nodding knowingly. "Superboy. The water tower stunt. I thought your mom was twigging onto me back there in the house."

"Were you in some accident, too? That's what they're really freaked out about," Piper said.

"Yeah," he said, "but it wasn't my fault. This little kid ran out in front of me and I jumped over a couple of parked cars to avoid him."

"On this scooter?"

"No," he shook his head. "Another one. A *former* scooter."

"But that's like those circus stunts," Piper said.

"That's what the newspaper story said," Judd admitted.

"But you did manage to avoid the kid and jump two parked cars. I'd think the paper would've called you a hero."

"Well . . . I didn't mention the *third* parked car. The *police* car," Judd said slowly.

"Oh," Piper said. "Judd, why didn't you *tell* me this?"

"Look . . . I understand. About tonight. About your folks. I mean, I know and you know I'm not a maniac. But as far as parents are concerned, *all* parents, I might as well be a teenage werewolf. I'm kind of getting used to it."

"Piper," her father called from the front porch.

"In a minute," she said, trying to stall him.

"Now," he said firmly.

"Look," she whispered to Judd, "I'll try to talk to them. Calm them down. Make them understand." She touched the spiky hair above his forehead, then added, "See you Monday. In homeroom."

She turned and ran back into the house. In the past ten minutes, her perfect world had collapsed into rubble.

Chapter 7

Piper woke up late the next morning, and at first snuggled back into "Saturday Glow" — the lazy, gradual realization that, at last, it was Saturday, the best day of the week. Then, with a jolt, she remembered the night before. Friday. Her great date. Judd. Her parents.

She moaned and pulled her pillow over her head to block out the world.

It was no use. She was wide awake. She'd have to get up and do her weekly chores — vacuuming the house, and cleaning the bathroom she shared with Molly, who, at nine, was already a hopeless slob. She would do the work because she had to, but she'd do it in total silence. There was no way she was going to talk to her parents today. Not after what they'd done to her the night before. Their words still rang in her ears.

"You are not to go out anywhere, not by

motorcycle, foot, or ox cart, with that ir-responsible lunatic," her father had told her after Judd had gone.

"He is *not* a lunatic," she had said, try-ing to defend him, to re-open the conversa-tion.

"Case closed," her mother had said, firmly shutting it. "I've heard a lot about that boy . . . all bad."

In response, Piper had turned, stomped up to her room, and stayed there for the rest of the night. Even when her mother came up later to try to explain again how all this was because they loved her so much. Even when her dad came up with a big bowl of popcorn, and asked her to come downstairs and watch *Friday Night Videos* with him. They were so hip and cool when it didn't matter. Then when it did, they turned into total old fogeys.

By the time Piper got dressed and went downstairs in the morning, everyone else was done with breakfast. Her mother was gone with the car — grocery shopping probably. Her dad had started in on the garage with Molly helping him paint the low trim. It was a perfect California day with clear blue skies and wall-to-wall sun. Piper just wished she were in a mood to enjoy it.

"I hope no one around this house is harboring any resentments," her dad shouted toward the kitchen window when he heard her rattling around inside, making a fresh pot of coffee. She didn't give him the satisfaction of a response. At the moment, she felt like she could be one of those nuns who don't speak to anyone for their whole lives.

"Daddy says you should just lighten up and get a new boyfriend," Molly said innocently, trying to be helpful.

Hearing this, Piper felt like a cartoon character. Her eyes felt like they were about to go "boing!" Her ears felt like they were about to start spouting steam.

New boyfriend! As if boyfriends were like pocket combs. If you lost one, you just stopped by the drugstore and picked up another. Well, Judd was the boyfriend she wanted, and Judd was the boyfriend she was going to have.

She got some milk out of the refrigerator and tried to think who she could talk to about all of this. Who knew how special Judd was? Who might help her with the secret relationship it looked like she and Judd were going to have to have?

Tamara! she thought, and went to the phone to call her. Then she remembered she didn't know Tamara's number, didn't even know her last name. Oh, well, Piper knew where she lived; they'd parted on her corner after their talk at The Thermos.

She'd just moved into the old hacienda-style house on the edge of town.

When Piper was younger, she and her friends used to soap its windows the night before Halloween. No one had lived there for years and the place was said to be haunted. Not that Piper believed in ghosts anymore. She was way too mature and sophisticated for that. Still — she did feel a little edgy as she stood on the front steps of the hacienda pressing the raspy door buzzer.

Now, she jumped when a tall, older, stooped man — completely bald and wearing a tuxedo — opened the door.

"Yesssss?" he said, eyeing her suspiciously.

"Uh . . . is Tamara here?" Piper asked softly.

The man arched an eyebrow and looked like he wanted to take her fingerprints, and run a lie detector test on her — for starters.

"Whommm may I say is calling?"

"Uh . . . just say Piper Davids. A friend of hers from school. But, I could come back some other time if. . . ."

"Please. This way," he said, ushering her through a dark hallway into an even darker, book-lined library. He pointed to an ancient red leather sofa. "Please sit. I will call her." And with that, he backed out of the room and was gone.

Piper looked around. All the books were in matching leather covers and looked like no one had read them in a hundred years. The room looked more like a movie set, like the library where James Bond meets the insane billionaire villain, than like an actual room in someone's actual house.

Suddenly the door opened again and there was Tamara. She was wearing a skirt and a silk blouse.

"Oh," Piper said. "Are you on your way out?"

"No. I was just reading."

She sure is dressed up just to be hanging around the house, Piper thought. Maybe she doesn't have any American-style casual clothes. Maybe she needed help picking some out. Piper tried to think of a way to ask about this.

"I am surprised to see you here, paying me this visit," Tamara was saying now, in her odd, formal way. Piper was getting to know her, though, and could tell she was pleased. "Tell me how your date was yesterday evening."

"Oh, Tamara! It was so horrible!" Piper wailed and almost instantly disintegrated into tears as she related the events of the night before.

"Oh, my," Tamara said, offering a delicate linen handkerchief, and placing a comforting hand on Piper's shoulder. "This is extremely terrible. Of course, my parents are also very strict. They would have done the same thing."

"Uh, was that your dad who brought me here?" Piper asked, sniffling.

"Tomás?! My father?!" For some reason, this struck Tamara as hilarious. When she stopped laughing, she said, "No, he is . . . he is my *uncle*."

"Oh," Piper said, not geting the joke. Actually, she didn't really understand a lot of what was going on in the house.

The library door opened again, and a youngish woman carrying a vase of fresh-cut flowers came into the room saying, "And where would you like me to put these, Your H — " She stopped in midsentence when she saw Piper. "Oh, I did not know we had company."

"Maria, this is my friend Piper. From school. Piper, this is Maria." Almost as an afterthought, Tamara added, "My *aunt*."

"Hi," Piper said and smiled, wondering if this aunt could be the wife of the old bald uncle. Maybe they were older brother and much younger sister. They didn't look anything like each other, and neither of them looked like Tamara. Who, in turn, didn't look anything like Adolfo — who came through the door now.

"Ah, a surprise guest," he said darkly. Piper was beginning to feel even more uncomfortable. Like one of those people on the phone company ads who should have called first.

"Well . . ." Piper said, looking at her watch. "I really have to get going."

"Oh, no," Tamara said. "You must stay and have tea with me — in the garden." She gestured with an airy motion toward the French doors at the end of the library.

"Uh, well, okay," said Piper, who liked new experiences. Tea? She followed Tamara out through the French doors, into a walled garden. It was the most marvelous place. Bright flowers grew everywhere, and near the back was a small fountain with waters splashing, almost musically. In the center was a white wicker table and chairs, where Tamara motioned to Piper that they should sit.

"It's almost . . . I don't know . . . a magical kind of place," Piper said, then laughed, a little embarrassed at herself. But she really was impressed. She'd never seen anything like this garden. Around Fairwood, most people had a backyard with a picnic table, a grill, and a swing set.

"Thank you," Tamara said, and smiled. "I also like it."

The next surprise was the tea. Piper was expecting a hot drink in a cup, not a whole meal. And what Tamara's Aunt Maria brought out on a heavy silver tray wasn't just an ordinary meal, either. More like a meal for the world's pickiest eater. Everything was small and a delicacy of some kind. Little sandwiches of smoked salmon, or caviar. Warm biscuits with a dish of homemade jam. Miniature eclairs and cream puffs.

"Mmmm," said Piper, blotting her mouth on a heavy linen napkin after sampling a few goodies. "This is *great*." She looked around. "Am I going to get to meet your parents today? What are they like?" Piper stopped. She could see that she was making Tamara nervous with all these questions. "Sorry. It's just that I really know so little about you. And I'm just a naturally curious person."

"My parents are back in Capria. I am here with Adolfo. We are living with our aunt and uncle, to experience American life, to get a wider view of the world," Tamara said.

"Well, I don't know how wide a view you'll get from Fairwood," Piper said thoughtfully. She had lived here all her life, and would have loved to see something else. "Tell me what it's like in Capria, what your life there is like."

Tamara paused, once again seeming to grope for just the right words.

"My life there is not typical, it is not the life of the ordinary Caprian girl. My home is high on a mountain. You can practically see the whole country from my window. My family . . . well, we have a life based on many traditions. My life is much like my mother's life, and her mother's before her. Things must be done just so. Certain clothes worn for certain occasions. Certain subjects learned. At a dinner party, I must make certain conversation."

"Doesn't sound like you have much fun," Piper said, biting into a mysterious, but delicious, sandwich.

"No, it is not fun. I do not have fun, I have responsibilities," Tamara answered seriously.

"What responsibilities?" Piper persisted.

"Oh, Piper," Tamara said, her shoulders heaving with a great sigh. "It is too hard to keep the truth from you."

"You mean I'm sticking my nose in your business . . . and I shouldn't."

"Nose?" Tamara said.

"Never mind!" Piper said. "What I mean is you feel I'm prying. And I shouldn't."

"No. I meant you are the only friend I have here, and I want you to know who I am. And yet. . . ." Tamara stopped and seemed to be wondering whether or not to reveal herself. She looked around the garden. Finally she threw up her hands and blurted out, "Oh all right. I am, you see — a princess."

Piper swallowed the sandwich she'd been munching and said, "I'm sorry. I must've heard you wrong."

"No. You heard me quite right. I am a princess — Her Royal Highness Tamara of Capria, to be exact. In my small country my parents are the king and queen. I live in a castle."

"Oh, my," Piper said and put down her plate.

"This is my secret. I am afraid that if people around here know, they will treat me differently, that they will find me . . . how do you say?" Tamara hesitated.

"Peculiar?" Piper offered.

"Yes. That is why the servants are posing as my aunt and uncle. And Adolfo is trying to seem like my brother, although I fear everyone knows already that he is my bodyguard."

"A princess," Piper gushed in spite of herself. "Wow."

"Does it make *you* think I'm peculiar?" Tamara asked.

Piper paused for a moment. It *was* a pretty stupendous piece of news. But she could see that it was important to Tamara that Piper *didn't* find her peculiar. And so she tried her best to act casual, to make it seem like every other day or so, one or another of her friends turned out to be a princess.

"Of course I don't think you're peculiar. At least not *so* peculiar. Everybody's peculiar in their own way. Yours is that you're a princess. So. . . ." Piper stopped suddenly and looked Tamara hard in the eye. "Say, now that I know, I'm not going to have to curtsy in front of you, or call you Your Royal Majesty or whatever?"

"Do not be ridiculous," Tamara said laughing. Then she said seriously, "But you *will* keep my secret?!"

"Of course. You're my best friend in homeroom."

"Yes?" Tamara was delighted.

Piper nodded, then mused, "It's funny. I made up my mind that we'd be friends that very first day in homeroom."

"You did?" Tamara said.

"I thought we have practically the same hair — except mine is blonde and yours is black. And we're practically the same size — great for trading clothes. And we agree on boys. That is, you agree with me that Judd is cute."

"And so is the Coach Talbot," Tamara said.

"Oh," Piper laughed. "Right."

"I am studying the American game of

59

football," Tamara confided, picking up a paperback book, *Football Made Easy*, off the table, and showing it to Piper. "So that I will have a subject of conversation with him."

"Oh, Tamara, you're something else!" Piper exclaimed, then thought for a minute. "You *are* something else — you're a real-life princess."

Tamara blushed. "You *do* think I'm odd."

"No, really I don't," Piper assured her. "It's just going to take a little getting used to. And it does kind of bring up about a million questions."

"Like?"

"Well, like do you usually wear a crown? Do you sit on a throne? Do you have all your dresses made by the royal dressmaker and all your jam made by the royal jam-maker — all that royal stuff?"

Tamara laughed. "Those *are* a lot of questions. Like my questions about American life. I don't think they can all be answered at once. Perhaps you should make a list for me."

Piper smiled. "Okay, you're on." Then her smile disappeared and a sad expression came over her face.

"You are thinking about your parents and Judd again?" Tamara asked.

"I don't know what I'm going to do,"

Piper said. "No sooner do I finally meet a boy I really like, than my parents tell me he's the one boy I can have nothing to do with."

"Perhaps you can find a way around their rules," Tamara said. "Perhaps you can find a way to have a romance *without* dating."

"I don't know how you do that," Piper said, shaking her head. "About all we have left together then is homeroom. And about all we can do in there is say hi and pass notes while Talbot reads the announcements."

"Notes are a little thing," Tamara said. "But they are *something*."

"Will you keep on being our postman?" Piper asked.

"Of course," Tamara said, smiling. "I am very interested in romance. I am a student of romance, you might say. This will be part of my homework."

"Good. I guess notes are better than nothing." Piper peered at what she was eating. "By the way, what's in this sandwich?"

Tamara looked closely. "Ah, a delicacy from our Caprian waters — curried eel."

Piper gulped.

"Now," Tamara said, pulling her notebook off the table. "Can you help me a little?"

"Shoot, Princess," Piper said. Tamara gave Piper a frightened look.

"Okay, just teasing," Piper said. "I promise to only call you Tamara."

"Thank you," Tamara said. "Now, on to important matters. What, please, is the meaning of 'shut your face'? I heard this during change of classes yesterday."

Piper tried to explain. "Well, it's kind of like asking someone to be quiet . . . but not quite."

When they were through with their tea and standing on the front steps of the old hacienda, Piper asked Tamara, "What do you say we get you a pair of jeans?"

"Jeans?" Tamara said, considering the possibility. "Yes, that would be interesting, I think."

"Good. We'll go out to the mall after school one day next week."

"Ah," Tamara said, smiling in anticipation. "Finally I will get to see *the mall*."

Chapter 8

On Monday, room 434 had some new decorations. Two big posters — "Yarmouth for Class President" — each with a photo of T. Craig in his trademark suspenders. In one picture, he was on the phone, looking intent on some important conversation. In the other, he was listening seriously to a gathering of students. The candidate himself, in person, was greeting every student in the homeroom as they came through the door.

"T. Craig Yarmouth. Vote for me."

"Why should I?" asked Eddie Baker, as T. Craig grabbed his hand to shake it heartily.

"Because I'll bring your issues to the student board. I'll be your friend in student government. Go ahead. Tell me. What do *you* want to see happen here at Fairwood High?"

Eddie didn't hesitate. "They should let

us wear our Walkmen during boring classes. And the principal and all the teachers should be forced to eat the cafeteria food."

"All *right*!" shouted several kids in the class and a general round of applause went up. T. Craig stood silent as everyone ignored him. He gathered up his courage again and turned to shake hands with the next person through the door. Unfortunately it was Tiffany Taylor — his main opponent in the class president race.

"Oh, Tiffany," he said, while she took back her hand cautiously, as though he had a creeping skin condition. "I've been wanting to talk with you." He lowered his voice and went on. "I think maybe we can work out something between us."

"Like what?" Tiffany said, extremely dubious.

"Well, I've been thinking," he said in his smoothest manner, "why should we fight each other on this? Why not work *together*?"

"Together?" she said, now downright suspicious.

"Yes. Split the ticket. Me for president, you for vice-president. An unbeatable combination, don't you think? United we stand, divided — "

"Divided *I* stand quite a good chance of being class president myself," Tiffany said crisply, then added as she walked to her desk, "Get real, T. Craig."

Piper had been determined to get to homeroom early so she could talk to Judd. But she was ten minutes late. She'd looked for Judd on the campus lawn, and all the way through the halls. Just in case he was late, too. But when she came into 434, there he was. She saw him right away, in spite of the fact that he was slumped dejectedly in the farthest desk in the corner. He looked up when she came in, but he didn't smile. Things were worse than she thought. She'd have to do something to let him know that, no matter what her parents thought, *she* didn't believe he was a dangerous character.

"Okay, okay," Coach Talbot was saying from the front of the room. "Let's get organized here. Into your seats, guys. That includes you, Big Shot," he said to T. Craig. "And girls — ladies — if you would please be seated."

Tamara, who'd been sitting in *her* desk for twenty minutes, who had in fact been the first one to arrive in 434 that morning, sighed. Coach Talbot was such a gentleman toward the girls. *Courtly* almost. With his manners, he'd fit right into her life back home. Perhaps. . . .

She was stopped in the middle of this thought by a tap-tapping on her arm. She turned. It was Piper. She'd been so absorbed in the coach that she hadn't even seen Piper come in. Tamara smiled across the aisle. Piper smiled back, then winked (what a strange American gesture this winking was!) and handed her a small, folded piece of paper.

"Postman?" she whispered.

Tamara nodded and passed the note toward the back of the room, indicating to Tiffany, whom she handed it to, that it was to go to Judd.

"Oh, how *junior high*," Tiffany said with disgust. "Passing notes. Kid stuff!" But she passed it on anyway, much to the relief of Piper, who watched the note's progess until she saw it safely reach Judd's hand.

He opened it to read:

No matter what my parents think, I trust you. But are you still interested in someone who's this much trouble?

He looked up, smiled across the room and nodded vigorously. *Yes!*

"Thanks, Judd," Coach Talbot said, misinterpreting Judd's enthusiastic nod. "I knew I could count on at least one brave soul to volunteer."

"Uh?" Judd said. "Just what was it I volunteered for?"

"Ms. Creedy's first aid class needs a victim to practice on. It's only for six weeks. This week, they'll be trying tourniquets and snake-bite measures on you. Have fun."

Judd sputtered helplessly, "But . . . wait. . . ."

"Next," the coach went on, "I need volunteers to be this month's homeroom monitors. To get here early and open the windows and straighten the desks, to stay late and erase the blackboards and collect lost articles. Anybody interested?" Not a hand went up. "Don't everybody rush in at once," he kidded.

Suddenly it occurred to Piper that this would be a perfect way for her and Judd to spend at least a few minutes each day together, alone. She shot her hand into the air.

Too late. The coach had given up on getting any volunteers, and was scanning the class list.

"Okay, nonvoluntary volunteers for September class monitors, Edward Baker and . . . Karen Murchinson."

Two simultaneous groans came from opposite sides of the room. From the last two people in 434 who wanted to spend time together each day — alone.

"Next," Coach Talbot said, shuffling through his sheaf of announcements. "Fairwood's annual Fall Frolic dance will be held on September twentieth in that romantic nightspot — *the gym*. Tickets go on sale this week and can be purchased...."

The Fall Frolic! Piper thought. The big mixer of the season. A *non-date* dance. Her parents would hardly keep her from going. And once she was there, she could dance the night away with Judd! The world suddenly seemed a little brighter.

"Do you want to be on the committee for decorations?" Tamara asked Piper after the bell had rung and they were gathering up their books and heading off to classes. "Something for friends to do together?"

Piper smiled. "Great. Yes," she told Tamara, putting an arm around her shoulders. "Something for friends to do together."

Cathy and Casey were the first ones out the door. They huddled around Cathy's open locker whispering as they watched the others, especially Piper, file out.

"I overheard her talking to The Spy," Casey said. "It seems Piper's parents don't like Judd too much. They think he's too dangerous for their little girl. Now she's forbidden to see him. Kind of puts a damper on their budding romance."

"Boo-hoo," Cathy said.

"My sentiments exactly. Anyway, now we've got the perfect opportunity to get her out of the picture — and someone much more deserving of Judd into it."

"We've *got* to get a sample of her handwriting," Cathy said.

"But how?" Casey wondered.

"I have French next period with her," Cathy mused. "Maybe I could just. . . ."

"Right," Casey said. "Do it. Meanwhile, I'm going to have a talk with the Incredible Hulk." She nodded toward Adolfo, who was leaning against a wall in the main corridor, watching over Tamara as usual. "See what I can find out about their spy ring. Life is certainly interesting!"

"For you," Cathy said. "How come you get to go after Judd and talk to spies, and that kind of thing, and all I do is get handwriting samples?"

"Don't whine," Casey said. "Just do it!"

Chapter 9

Mr. Laurent bounded into the class room, late as usual, his tie flying out behind him like a thin banner. This tie was rose-colored. Mr. Laurent's shirt was navy. His pants were pale green and extremely baggy, wrinkled and unstructured. Mr. Laurent was French and, to Piper's thinking, about six times more stylish than anyone else within miles of Fairwood.

"*Alors*," he said, running both his hands through his hair. "Today we continue with the present tense. Has everyone prepared for the dialogue, 'Jean and Françoise Go to the Post Office'?"

Piper groaned silently. She loved listening to Mr. Laurent speak French. She even had secret dreams of an older version of herself speaking as fluently as he did, laughing at witty little French jokes told by her chic French friends as they all sat in a café sipping café au lait. But she absolutely hated French class with its boring dialogues and beginning students murdering the language in their unique ways.

"Bon-jur, Frankoize," one of them was reading now. Piper looked up. Cathy Connor. No one murdered French quite as gruesomely as Cathy did.

Mr. Laurent corrected her in his kind way, and none of the other kids laughed at her. Everyone was scared that they sounded as bad themselves. They all reluctantly took their turns pretending to be either Jean or Françoise, buying stamps, looking in their postal box, and mailing a letter to their cousin Hector in the United States.

It was *so* boring. Try as she might, Piper couldn't keep her attention focused. She was helpless against the pull of other thoughts. Thoughts about Judd. A terrific fantasy in which his daredevil nature paid off. Some little kid was drowning way out in the middle of Higgins Lake outside of town. She and Judd were on the beach and he spotted the kid going down for the second time. He leaped up and into the water, swam through the surf, fought off a circle of hovering sharks, and carried the kid back to shore. Everyone on the beach applauded. The local TV station came with a mini-cam truck to interview him, and Piper's parents were forced to change their opinion of him.

She realized this was a stupid fantasy. For one thing there weren't any sharks or surf in dinky Higgins Lake. But still, Piper was enjoying herself with it, when she felt a finger jabbing at her shoulder blade. She looked up and saw that the bell had rung and the class was filing out of the room. She turned around to see who'd been poking her. Cathy Connor.

"Say," Cathy said. "I lost my vocabulary words from last week, see, and I was wondering if I could borrow yours and copy them?"

"Uh, sure," Piper said, leafing through her notebook to find the right page.

"That'll do," Cathy said.

"*These* are verb conjugations," Piper said.

"Oh, yeah. Right," Cathy said, looking around the room as if she was bored with waiting. As if she was doing Piper a favor instead of the other way around.

Still, Piper couldn't think of any reason not to give her the list. That would just be mean. Finally she found it.

"Thanks," Cathy said, practically ripping the sheet of paper out of Piper's hand. "I'll get it back to you tomorrow." And she ran toward the door.

"So nice getting a chance to talk with you, Cathy," Piper called sarcastically to the twin, who was already out of the class-room door, on her way to find her sister.

During second period, Tamara had cooking. The king and queen had insisted on this, as she had never in her life so much as boiled an egg.

"But we have a chef!" she had protested to her father. "I will always have a chef! It is foolish for me to waste time learning a skill I will never use."

"Perhaps someday you will be ship-wrecked on a desert island with only an egg and a pot, and the chef will have gone down with the ship." Her father, although you'd never guess it from his public image, could be funny when he wanted to.

Tamara had to laugh in spite of herself when the first day's lesson had been "Boiling an Egg." Hers had turned out kind of green in the middle with an extremely rub-bery white part. She had hoped they would have a class in hors d'oeuvres, particularly recipes featuring caviar and quail eggs. And she'd been hoping she'd learn to roast a pheasant, her favorite dish. But Ms. Finster had been quite sarcastic when Tamara had suggested the pheasant proj-ect. Instead, she had the class fix one inedi-ble dish after another.

What, for instance, were these things called pancakes? Flat, fried, doughy slabs to be covered with sap from a tree? And macaroni and cheese — what a disgusting, gooey mess! Especially her potful.

And to make things worse, she had to face this dismal class at ten in the morning. Back home at that hour, she was just being gently wakened by Maria with a pot of freshly ground coffee and a hot croissant.

"Today, we're making Sloppy Joes," Ms. Finster was saying now. Tamara had been wondering about these Joes ever since she saw them on the schedule.

"Start by putting your oil and onions into your pans, then adding your ground meat and browning it," Ms. Finster said to the twelve students standing in pairs at their stoves.

Tamara's class partner was Eddie Baker, who was as bad, no, possibly worse, at cooking than she was. Tamara turned to him now and asked, pointing at the package of meat, "This is Joe?"

Eddie started laughing, at first just a little, then harder. The harder he tried to keep from laughing in the middle of class, the harder he laughed.

Tamara tried to distract him. "Come. Let us begin this browning. What is *browning*, anyway?"

He shook his head and stared at the recipe as if it was written in another language.

"Not sure," he said and shrugged. "I hope it's like burning, since that seems to be our main cooking technique. I hate to say this, Tamara, but I hope you and I don't ever fall in love and wind up marrying each other. Dinnertime would be pretty depressing."

Now it was Tamara's turn to laugh. The idea of her and Eddie falling in love was ludicrous. Of them cooking dinner together. Of Eddie being the new prince, greeting visiting dignitaries in his leather jacket, his one earring, and his surly glare. This made her laugh even harder.

"Don't mind me," Eddie said finally. "I just stopped by to brown some hamburger."

"Excuse me," Ms. Finster said from the stove at the front of the class. "But I believe this is cooking class, not comedy class."

Tamara and Eddie tried to put on their most serious expressions.

Tamara was confused by Eddie. She suspected that underneath his tough act, there was a lot more going on. She also hoped that because he was so odd himself, he wouldn't find *her* odd, or wouldn't mind that she was odd. He treated her just like he would've treated anyone who'd been assigned as his cooking partner — that is, with relentless sarcasm.

"Now pour in your tomato sauce," Ms. Finster was saying. Tamara watched Eddie do this, and the two of them stood over their pan, watching the sauce bubble like a witch's cauldron, and then get crusty and burnt around the edges.

"No hot cooking!" Ms. Finster shouted as she came across the room toward them, waving her wooden spoon. "I said simmer those Joes, not *incinerate* them!"

Tamara looked around. The other teams were ladling out nice warm spoonfuls of Sloppy Joe onto opened buns, while she and Eddie tried to calm down their wildly smoking pan. Finally he just poured a huge jug of water into the hissing mess and they both looked gloomily down at what was surely another F.

"Hey," he said when they were washing the dishes. "I wanted to tell you to watch out for the twins."

"Why?" Tamara asked. "I hardly know them."

"I spotted Casey cornering your brother in the hallway when I came in here. I overheard her and her sister talking the other day. They think there's something suspicious about you. Because you're foreign, I guess. Anyway, I don't know what they're up to, but my guess is it's no good."

"Thank you for telling me, Eddie," Tamara said seriously.

"No problem," he said. "Hey. Do you think Finster would let us just work with a microwave? I think maybe we could handle that."

At lunchtime, Adolfo caught up with Tamara and told her about his conversation with Casey.

"This twin girl waited until everyone was into the classrooms. Then she made a sneaky move up beside me and told me 'hi.' "

"Very friendly," Tamara said sarcastically.

"But *I* was not," Adolfo said. "And when she said to me, 'You don't seem to have many classes,' I did not even bother replying."

"And then?" Tamara said.

"Then she said, 'Or do you just wait for your *sister*? If she really *is* your sister. I must say you two don't look at all alike.' At this point I had had enough. I turned and looked down at her and told her, 'Oh, you are too clever for us. You have discovered our secret, that Tamara and I are psychologists from another planet, studying your species. Our special assignment is *twins*. First we must observe them in their natural habitat, *then* take them on board with us, back to our galaxy.' "

Tamara smiled. "What did she say to this?"

"I think she wasn't sure I was making it up. At any rate, she became very nervous and said she had to be going and would 'see me around.' I said, 'Oh, no, little twin. It is *we* who will see *you* around!'"

He looked at Tamara and confessed, "It is the first time I have had a good laugh since I came here. I hope you think I did the right thing, Your Highness."

"You were perfect, Adolfo. Just perfect. I will tell my father and I'm sure he will reward you."

Chapter 10

"Hey," Piper said, coming up behind Tamara as she was putting her books onto the shelf of her locker. "Want to go to the mall today?"

Tamara turned, her eyes wide. "We can get my jeans?"

"And a sweatshirt," Piper said. "I'll bet you don't have one of those, either."

"A shirt for sweating," Tamara made a face. "I think this grosses me out."

Piper tried to cover her smile with her hand, but she wasn't fast enough.

"I said it wrong?" Tamara asked.

"No, no. You said it fine," Piper assured her. "I guess it was just *you* saying it at all that's funny."

"Well, I must practice if I am ever going to sound like a regular American girl. So now let us shut our faces, please, and go!"

* * *

"So many stores in one place!" Tamara said, looking up and around from the middle of the mall's plaza.

"We can start at my favorite," Piper said, leading Tamara over to a shop called Elle. When they were at the door, Piper turned and asked Tamara, "How much can you afford to spend? Do you get, like, an allowance or anything? From your parents?"

Tamara opened her wallet and pulled out a credit card. "They just let me use this. It is good here?"

"Oh, yes," Piper laughed. "Very good. This is definitely the most amazing thing about you. Forget that you're a princess. That's small stuff compared to the fact that your parents *gave* you a credit card!"

"It just makes it so much easier to buy the things I want," Tamara said innocently.

"I'll have to put it that way to my parents," Piper joked. "I'm sure they'll see the light."

When they were inside the store, Tamara looked around, and wailed to Piper. "But how will I ever choose?! There must be a thousand jeans in here!"

"Well, you have to decide first what your style is. For you, I'd say definitely designer. . . ."

"No," Tamara said firmly. "I want to

look like a regular American teenage girl."

No small task, Piper thought as she looked hard at Tamara — at her deeply-pleated white trousers and white silk shirt, and delicate white sandals. If there was anything she did *not* look like, it was a regular American teenage girl. More like a grown-up European movie star. But she tried anyway.

"Okay, then you'll be wanting stone-washed jeans, and a sweatshirt like this — *royal* blue, definitely your color," Piper teased, as she pulled these items off the stacks piled high on the store's shelves. "But for starters, you should probably get rid of these," she said, looping a finger through the strand of pearls at Tamara's neck.

"May I help you?" a familiar voice said. They both turned to see Tiffany Taylor, who was wearing an "Elle — My Name Is Tiffany" plastic badge on her sweater.

"I didn't know *you* worked here," Piper said.

"Just started this week," Tiffany said. "I'm in desperate need of the bucks." Her voice sounded glum. "It's going to take up most of the time I need for the campaign, though. T. Craig's rich; he doesn't have to do anything after school except shake people's hands."

"So?" Piper said. "Let him."

"What?" Tiffany said.

"Most of the kids are sick of his campaigning already. Let him burn out. Then, just before the election, step in and be the fresh face. I'll help." Piper hadn't liked T. Craig since that first time he'd called Judd "Superboy."

"I will help also," said Tamara, who liked Tiffany. She was the only person in school who dressed remotely like Tamara.

"But how can you help?" Tiffany said.

"Well," Piper said, "Tamara and I seem to be the entire decoration committee for the Fall Frolic. Whatever *we* want is what goes up on those walls for the big night. If there were a couple of Tiffany Taylor posters there among all those construction-paper leaves, it might be like subliminal psychological advertising. Put you in people's minds without them even knowing it. And just four days before the election."

"You guys!" Tiffany said. "It sounds good." Then they all heard someone clearing his throat behind them. The store manager. Tiffany changed her manner dramatically and put on her strictly business persona.

"So, ladies, how may I help you today?"

"Well, we'd like some rowdy jeans and sweats for my friend here," Piper said, indicating Tamara.

"Jeans and sweats?!" Tiffany said. "But

that's not your style at all, Tamara. You have this terrific elegance about you. Like some fairytale princess or something. . . ."

Tamara was speechless. Piper rushed in to smooth out the awkward moment.

"Uh . . . well, that's just the look she wants to get rid of. Tired of it. This is the sort of look she's after," Piper said, holding out the stone-washed jeans and blue sweatshirt.

"But then you'll just look like everyone else at Fairwood," Tiffany said despairingly.

"Precisely," Tamara said, smiling.

"Now we can look for something for you," Tamara said, when they'd bought the jeans and sweatshirt and were sitting on a bench by the jewelry booth in the middle of the mall.

"Oh, no," Piper said. "I can't afford a thing."

"Oh. You are broken," Tamara said.

"You mean broke," Piper corrected her. "No, I'm worse than broke. I'm in debt. Last week I even borrowed money from one of the kids I babysit for. Talk about desperate. No, the best thing you could do, as a true friend, is keep me out of *all* stores."

"But we can shop the windows?" Tamara asked.

"Window shop? Sure. That doesn't cost

a thing. And that way you can see the rest of the mall."

After they'd walked around for an hour or so, Piper led Tamara to her favorite silly spot in the mall.

"Twenty-four Carrot?" Tamara said, puzzled as she read the sign.

"It's a health food restaurant and juice bar. It has twenty-four flavors of fruit and vegetable juices."

"Ah, do you think they have Caprian fippleberry?"

"Uh . . . I doubt it," Piper said. "But come in anyway. It's kind of a weird place, but I like it."

Inside, Tamara was delighted by the stools, which were shaped like mushrooms, and the tables, which had orange carrot-shaped pedestals with green glass tops. The counter people all wore hats shaped like bunches of broccoli.

"This is most wonderful!" Tamara exclaimed. She ordered a glass of gooseberry juice, which she thought was closest to her native fippleberry juice. Piper had her favorite — carrot-celery juice. Weird, but great. They'd barely been sitting for two minutes when Judd walked in. Piper was totally surprised to see him there, and totally shocked to see that his head was wound in a big bandage.

"Judd!" she said, rushing over to him. "Are you all right?"

He nodded and knocked the side of his head with his knuckles.

"But I'll tell you, those first aid students are a dangerous bunch. They definitely can't be let loose on sick people. Look what they did to someone who was perfectly well."

They sat him down and ordered him a giant-sized glass of the house special Health Jolt, and then nearly fell off their mushrooms laughing as he told the story.

"They had my arm in a sling and my snake bite all tourniqueted. I thought I was home free. But I hadn't counted on them dropping my stretcher on the way to the ambulance."

He told them that, under all the bandaging, there was only a small cut.

"They wanted to take care of it themselves. I told them over my dead body, and then realized that probably wasn't the threat to use with them. Anyway, I got them to take me to the school nurse and she patched me up. Even *she* said I probably shouldn't let them near me again, if I can help it."

"What's this?!" he said next, after he'd tasted his first sip of the Health Jolt. "Now I'm being poisoned!" He grabbed his throat in mock strangulation.

The three of them were laughing and fooling around so much that they didn't see who was approaching until she was standing over them. It was Piper's mother's best friend, Brenda Williams.

"Hi, Pipesqueak," she said, using her old-time nickname for Piper.

"Hi, Brenda," Piper said, then before she thought better, introduced Tamara and Judd to her. Suddenly Brenda's friendliness chilled a bit, just enough for Piper to notice. For a second she couldn't figure out why, and then suddenly she realized it was Judd. Her mother had told Brenda about him, what a menace to society he was. And now Brenda was going to go straight home, call Piper's mother, and tell her who she'd just run into. By the time Piper got home she was going to be in deep trouble.

Piper looked at Judd's bandage and felt her stomach flip. Her mother would surely think Judd had been climbing water towers again. No doubt about it, she and Judd were doomed.

Besides, she'd never be able to make her mother believe that running into Judd had been purely accidental. She felt queasy watching her immediate future unfold before her eyes with no way of stopping the sickening chain of events.

Chapter 11

The next morning Karen dragged her feet the whole way to school, but still wound up there at eight-fifteen, right on time to begin her assignment as homeroom monitor. She was just dreading it. She could barely stand to be around Eddie even when 434 was full of kids. Alone together every morning, there'd be no hiding from his little snubs and cutting remarks. She still had one small hope left as she came through the still quiet school corridors. Maybe he wouldn't show up. After all, Eddie was a punk-out specialist.

But when she came through the door to room 434, there he was, furiously erasing the blackboard.

"Really throwing yourself into your work, I see," Karen said.

But he didn't so much as acknowledge her presence; just kept rubbing away at the blackboard.

"Eddie," Karen said, getting mad, "I'm *not* going to come here every morning for a month just to get the *silent* treatment from you. It's just *too* stupid."

He turned and gave her a cold look. "Why is it so stupid *now*? Last spring you made it pretty clear you didn't have anything more to say to me. Now all of a sudden you want to get chatty again. *Donnez-moi un* break, as the French would say."

"Look," Karen said, coming up to where he stood at the board, "I am going to be a *big* star and all. I just want to leave *everything* about my old life behind — and you, well, you just seem so *much* a part of it."

"You mean just because I don't want to be a movie star?"

"Because you don't want to be *anything*, or do *anything* except hang out in your garage listening to the radio, and fixing up that old Chevy. How you could spend *that* many hours lying underneath a car I *never* could understand."

"You never tried to understand. *I* tried to understand how you could spend so much of your time rehearsing those tiny roles you'd get in the community theater productions. I even helped you practice that maid's part — the one where all you got to say was, 'May I dust the parlor now, Madame?' '*May* I dust the parlor now,

Madame?' 'May *I* dust the parlor now, Madame?' 'May I *dust* the parlor now, Madame?' 'May I dust the *parlor* now, Madame?' 'May I dust the parlor *now*, Madame?' 'May I dust the parlor now, *Madame*?' "

Karen smiled in spite of herself, remembering how he had helped her rehearse this one stupid line for almost a whole night.

"You really *could* be sweet sometimes, Eddie Baker."

"Yeah?" he said, toughening. "Well, I'm through being sweet around you. It only seems to get me kicked in the teeth."

"Eddie . . . ?" Karen said, but he did not want to hear anything she had to say.

He put up a silencing hand and said, in a dead voice, "Better straighten those rows of desks. The mob'll be mobbing in here in about five minutes."

While Eddie and Karen were at odds in 434, Casey and Cathy were deep in conspiratorial conversation over at The Thermos, where they often stopped on the way to school in the mornings. Both of them believed that, even for the serious dieter, a good breakfast was essential.

"I can't believe you bought that story of his!" Cathy exclaimed as they both dug into plates of eggs, biscuits, and gravy. "Interplanetary psychologist, my eye!"

"I didn't say I *really* believed him," Casey said defensively. "Just that he was pretty scary saying it." She ate some of her eggs, then added huffily, "You weren't there. Now. Do we have the note with us?"

Cathy tapped her jacket pocket, smiled, and said, "Plan A — ready to go." Then, looking over at the dessert case on the counter, she asked her sister, "Do you think cherry pie is essentially the same as two slices of toast with jam?"

By the time Piper got to homeroom, the place was bustling. T. Craig was passing out copies of his position paper on burning student issues like off-campus lunch, public displays of affection in the halls, and making phys ed optional. Tiffany was passing out cardboard buttons she'd printed up saying, "Taylor is Tops."

Karen and Eddie were busy ignoring each other, the twins as usual were utterly absorbed in each other's conversation. What *did* they find to talk about all the time? Piper wondered. Tamara was up at Coach Talbot's desk, asking him about the Falcons' defensive strategy this season. She must've really studied up! Judd was sitting, his big bandage now down to just a

Band-Aid, in the back corner, watching the door for Piper. At least this was how it seemed to Piper as she came into the room. He was probably concerned about how things had gone with her parents after they'd heard from Brenda.

Actually, by the time Piper got home, the scene was much worse than she'd even anticipated. Not only had Brenda had time to call Piper's mother, but Piper's mother had had time to talk it over with Piper's dad.

"Oh, boy," Piper said as she came into the kitchen and saw the expressions on her parents' faces.

"You weren't supposed to see that boy again, Piper," her father said.

"I didn't see him," Piper answered.

"Oh, he's invisible?" Mr. Davids asked.

"And, obviously, he was in another accident," Mrs. Davids said. "Brenda said his head was all bandaged."

Piper sighed wearily. "We met by accident. He just happened to come into 24 Carrot. His head was bandaged because the first aid students dropped him while they had him on a stretcher." Piper groaned inwardly as she heard the story she was telling.

"Piper, that is the dumbest story I have ever heard," her father said. "And, your mother and I repeat, you are *not* to see this boy again. The next time, he'll involve you in his irresponsible accidents."

Then they sent her upstairs, and had Molly bring her supper up later. She hated this. The Frosty Treatment, she called it. In her opinion, it was the worst thing her parents did to her. It was like shutting her outside the family. And in this case — *it was completely unfair!*

And so now she desperately wanted to get to Judd before homeroom began, to tell him what had happened, and to let him know she wasn't giving up in spite of any of it.

But before she could make her way to the back of the room, Coach Talbot finished talking with Tamara and motioned the class to find their seats and quiet down for the day's announcements. Piper slumped into a desk in frustration, and almost immediately began trying to put the rush of things she had to say to Judd in a note.

My folks are furious and they're giving me the big cold shoulder. But I don't care. They're wrong about you, and I'm just going to have to prove it to them. In the meantime, I guess we'll have to be even more secret about seeing each other. I just hope this isn't

too much of a drag for you, and that
you don't go off and date someone else.
                        Piper

This was the note that Piper wrote, folded into little squares, and passed along to Tamara, who passed it along to Tiffany. But today Cathy Connor had taken the seat between Tiffany and Judd and, with a lightning-fast move, she slipped Piper's note into her right pocket while out of her left pocket she pulled out another, also on loose-leaf paper, also folded into little squares. This was the note she passed on to Judd. He opened it and read:

My parents had a long talk with me last night and what they said about you made sense. You're just too danger-ous. I need someone more stable. I'm considering T. Craig, who is already very corporate in spite of only being fifteen. My parents would like him much better. I think you need a girl-friend who's more like you, a little on the wild side. Someone whose parents don't keep a very close eye on her. I was thinking of Casey Connor. You've probably already thought of this obvi-ous choice yourself, but in case you hadn't, I thought I'd point out that

you two are practically made *for each
other. I hope in the future, you will
consider me your friend, but just your
friend — and not a friend you talk to
all that much.*

Pipper

Judd, thinking that Piper really had
written these words, was filled with disbelief, then rage. He looked up across the
room at her in spite of himself, and was
stunned to see that she was smiling at him.
How callous! Didn't she have any feelings
at all?! Here she was, shooting him down,
and smiling at him at the same time! He
took the note and, in a fast gesture of
anger, crumpled it, and threw it on the
floor.

Piper watched in bewilderment as he did
this. The hostile gesture must mean he was
sick of her and all the trouble her parents
were making for them. It didn't matter
that she was still willing to try to see him.
He was no longer interested in *her*.

She felt terrible, sick almost. She had
lost the one guy she'd ever wanted — *before* she'd had a chance to get him!

Chapter 12

By the end of the day, Piper didn't feel any better. If anything she felt *more* miserable. Anytime she got to feeling the slightest bit better, all she had to do was run through her mind again the tape of Judd's angry glare as he crushed her note in his fist.

She walked out of school at a snail's pace, her books feeling like a load of stone slabs in her arms. She walked to the nearest tree and sat down with her back against it, her head down. Anyone who looked close enough could see she was crying.

Tamara was, at that same moment, on the opposite end of the mood spectrum. She practically flew out of school, down the walk, and across the lawn to find Piper. When she did, she threw herself onto the ground next to her friend, rolled onto her back, and looked up at the fluffy clouds dotting the sky.

"Life is fluffy sometimes, like the little clouds, no?" she said in a dreamy way.

"Tamara, have you been sniffing the beakers in chemistry class?" Piper asked.

"I am just a very happy person today, as they say," Tamara said huffily.

"Let me guess," Piper said. "This mood couldn't possibly have anything to do with someone on our Fairwood faculty? Someone perhaps in the area of athletics? Someone like, oh, just taking a wild guess, Coach Talbot?"

"It is so wonderful! He has been assigned as chaperone for the Fall Frolic! My idea is that the music will be wonderful and he will want to waltz with someone, and who will be right there?" Answering herself unnecessarily, she added, "Me!"

"That's great," Piper said in a dead tone of voice.

"What is it?" Tamara asked. "You got a bad grade on your book report? Tommy Henderson wants you to pay him back all the money he has loaned you?" She paused. "It is about Judd, isn't it?"

At this Piper burst into tears. Tamara lent her another delicate linen handkerchief, put a comforting arm around her shoulders, and just sat there with Piper until she ran out of tears. When she did,

Tamara asked her to start at the beginning and tell the whole story.

When Piper was through, Tamara thought for a while in silence, then she said, "This does not make sense."

"What do you mean?" Piper said with slight irritation.

"This story — the pieces do not fit together. There was nothing in your note to make Judd angry. He might not want to continue in this way, with your parents so against him, but this would only make him frustrated, or maybe indifferent. But not angry."

"So what are you saying? You think he's some kind of nut case or something?"

"I have an idea," Tamara said mysteriously. "But there is something I must check before I draw any conclusions. And if you will excuse me, I think I must hurry."

"Tamara!" Piper protested. "Tell me what you're up to!"

Tamara stood to go, then held up a hand in a commanding way.

"Trust me. I will come to your house later. If I am right, I may have good news."

Something in Tamara's manner made Piper hopeful.

The first thing Tamara did when she left Piper under the palm tree was ask around about the twins.

"Have you seen them?" she asked Tiffany, who hadn't, then Karen, who was just coming out of the school's side door.

"Uh, yeah. I *think* they're down in the basement, by the vending machines."

Tamara rushed back into school and then down the side stairs, which came out behind the machines. When she pushed open the heavy metal door, she did it softly, and walked lightly so as not to be heard approaching. When she was a few feet away, on the other side of the bank of machines, she could hear them.

"If we have diet sodas," one twin said (it was hard to tell their voices apart), "then I think we can have some corn chips, too."

"And pizza," the other twin said, then started laughing. "I just can't stop thinking of the expression on his face."

"I'm worried we shouldn't have put in the part about me. I'd rather have him fall in love with me in this terrific flash of discovery. Although this will probably speed up the process. Maybe we should get home now. In case he's trying to call me," Casey said.

"Okay. Let me just get some candy."

Tamara backed up slowly and silently, until she could reach behind her and feel the metal door. Once safely on the other side of it, she ran as fast as she could, back up the stairs and along the long main corridor to the 400 wing. She ran like a shot down to the end and into 434, stumbling over desks as she went.

Since the room wasn't used for anything else all day, the debris from homeroom period was still there. She dropped to the floor and hunted around. Then she saw it laying under the desk where she'd remembered Judd sitting that morning. The note!

She opened it and read it in a rush. Then again, slowly, taking in every diabolical lie. She neatly folded it into fours and slid it into the back pocket of her new jeans and left the room. It was time to find Judd.

She rushed over to the football field and saw with relief that the team was still practicing. She couldn't tell which one was Judd, what with all the helmets and shoulder pads, but she knew he was out there somewhere. She would just have to wait until practice was over.

This was kind of a bonus since it gave her the opportunity to watch Coach Talbot at work. She still thought he was the most handsome male being around Fairwood High. And now that he knew she was interested in football, maybe he would see her as more than just another girl in homeroom.

Her fantasy at the moment was that he would look up, see her sitting in the stands, and wave. But this didn't happen. He was all business out on the field, "pushing the Falcons to their limits, and beyond," as he had been quoted in the school paper, the *Fairwood Free Press*.

Who *did* notice her was Judd. When practice was over, and the team was ambling off the field, pulling off their helmets and horsing around with each other as they headed for the locker room, he looked up and gave her a pathetic wave.

"I need to talk to you!" she shouted.

He looked doubtful, but he yelled back, "Meet me by the locker room door in ten minutes."

She could tell he had hurried to meet her. When he came out, his hair was still wet from the shower, and he'd gotten his T-shirt on inside out.

"What's up?" he asked as they walked together across the football field, now golden with the late afternoon sun washing across it.

"Piper didn't write this," she said, pulling the note out of her pocket.

"Where'd you get that?!" he said, shocked to see it again.

"Where you left it."

"It's in her writing. What makes you think she didn't write it?"

"Well, for one thing, I think Piper knows how to spell her own name." Tamara pointed to the signature, "Pipper."

"Could be a mistake," Judd said, still not convinced.

Tamara shook her head. "I just talked to her. She thinks *you've*, how do you say it?, dumped *her*."

Judd puzzled this out for a moment, then nodded. "But how could she think that?"

"I think she sent you a nice note and someone switched it to this nasty one. Then Piper saw your response to the nasty note and thought you were responding to the one *she* wrote. Not the fake note."

"But who wrote the fake one?" Judd asked.

"The twins, I think."

"You're right! That plug for Casey really gives them away. But how can we get back at them?"

"I have an idea. But first, I must go to Piper's house and explain all this to her. I hate thinking of her being as miserable as she is for one second longer. Then I will take care of the dirty mice."

"Rats," Judd corrected. "Dirty rats. And Tamara, will you ask Piper to call me tonight if she can? Or meet me somewhere?

I'd really like to talk to her someplace a little less . . . well, public, than homeroom. If you know what I mean."

Tamara smiled. "Yes, even though I have led a very sheltered life, I think I know what you mean."

Chapter 13

Tamara started running back across the school lawn on her way to Piper's house. Her long black hair flew behind her in the light wind. She felt fast and free in her jeans, and in her new persona. Here, where no one knew she was a princess, she didn't have to worry about acting proper and dignified. She could just be a regular, slightly rowdy sixteen-year-old.

Suddenly though, her path was blocked by a large hulking presence.

"Adolfo!" she said sharply. "Please. Out of my way. I am in a hurry."

"I will drive you where you are hurrying." He gestured toward the blue Mercedes parked at the far end of the school lot.

"You know I don't like you to bring the car here. It only calls attention to us."

"Then I will leave it and we will walk. Together."

"But don't you see, that is *worse*. It looks so odd, you always following me. Soon everyone will guess you are my body-guard."

"But that is my job. Come. No one is around anymore. It is almost five. They have all gone home. No one will see you are a princess who rides in a Mercedes."

Reluctantly she followed him, got into the back seat, pulled a bottle of sparkling water from the minifridge and turned on the small television. She was so used to traveling that way that she didn't even find it luxurious anymore. She had actually come to hate the Mercedes, to think of it as the "isolation capsule." Adolfo got into the front and started up the car. Then, when they were nearly to the exit, T. Craig and Tiffany came out of the school, carrying their posters from a student government forum.

They stood staring at the Mercedes and then, as the car passed by them, they looked in and saw Tamara. If only they had said something, anything, it would have been bearable for her. *Un*bearable were their silent stares.

Tamara waved a weak wave from her side of the tinted glass and watched as they returned with slow-motion waves of their own. But mostly they just stared. Like Tamara was a rare animal in the zoo. Some odd and different species, not at all like them. How could she ever be friends with them after they had looked at her like this?! Just when things seemed to be getting better, suddenly she felt once again shut outside.

She didn't speak to Adolfo until they were almost to Piper's house.

"Leave me here," she told him when they were still a block away. "I refuse to let you embarrass me again today by pulling up in my friend's drive."

As she got out and walked toward Piper's, Tamara tried to shrug off her bad mood. She had good news for her friend and didn't want to color it with her own shade of gray.

She rang the bell and waited, listening to the thudding of feet rushing down the stairs, and Piper's shout of, "I'll get it, Mom!"

She was breathless when she finally answered the door. And clearly happy to see Tamara.

"Good news?" she asked eagerly.

"Perhaps," Tamara teased her. "Maybe you will invite me in so that I can sit down and tell you this long story of good news."

"Oh, of course," Piper said. "Hey, I'll fix you homemade lemonade and Tollhouse cookies, and prop you up on the sofa, and fan you with a huge plume. If only you'll spill the beans!"

"Beans?" Tamara said, puzzled by yet another American expression.

"Never mind. Forget I said it," Piper said, showing Tamara up the stairs and to her room, turning down the Pretenders record on the stereo, and flopping onto her bed, while Tamara sat down on the chair at Piper's desk and told the whole story of her detective work on the twins, and her talk with Judd.

"He wants to see you tonight. Somewhere you can talk with privacy."

"Oh, no! Tonight I have to babysit for the Worst Children in the World." Piper thought a minute. "Could you call him and tell him to meet me there, at the Hendersons'? Say around nine? The little monsters ought to be in bed by then. I'll write down the address."

Piper scrawled the address and Judd's phone number on a piece of paper, as Tamara looked around at Piper's room — so different from her own. This room had not been done by royal decorators — or any decorators. Its decor was simply walls and surfaces filled with Piper's life. Snapshots of Piper and her family on vacation. Piper on waterskis. Photos of her favorite stars. A bookcase stuffed with twice as many books as it was built to hold. Tamara looked at all of this with longing.

"Now," Piper said, sitting up on her bed, wrapping her arms around her knees. "Speaking of evil children — what are we going to do about the twins?"

"I have a little plan," Tamara said, smiling slyly as she began to spell out the details to Piper. Tomorrow they would take care of Casey and Cathy. Tonight, Piper had more pleasant matters to attend to. Seeing Judd ... alone!

Geting all five Henderson kids — Tommy, Donny, Ronny, Connie, and Bonnie — to bed was like wrestling an octopus. As soon as Piper had them all in their beds with their teeth brushed and their night-lights on, one of them would want to get up for a drink of water. Then another had lost his stuffed bunny. And then by this time another had awakened from a bad dream.

Finally tonight, just before nine, Piper managed to get them all in bed and was pretty sure they were asleep. She stood very still at the bottom of the stairs to make absolutely sure. One weekend night around two A.M., she had been pretty sure they were asleep, but kept hearing little clicking noises and finally followed them up to the boys' room, where all five were under a huge tent of blankets, playing a marathon game of Monopoly by flashlight.

But now everything seemed to be truly quiet, and Piper went to the front window to wait for Judd. But when she pulled aside the drape and looked out, he was already there, leaning against his motor scooter. She motioned for him to come around to the side door.

She opened it, let him in, and pulled him into the Hendersons' pantry, but before she had a chance to say anything, he had his arm around her and was pulling her into a long, gentle hug.

When they finally both pulled back to look at each other, he said dramatically, "We are *never* going to let anyone or anything — not parents or crazy twins or tornadoes or hurricanes — keep us apart."

"Never *ever*," she agreed, and they were both very serious for a second or two. Then Judd's eyes started crinkling around the corners and Piper knew a joke was coming.

"Boy, I thought this dating was going to be a breeze," he said. "Nobody told me it's such hard work!"

"But we haven't even gotten to the dating part yet," Piper pointed out. "Probably won't until I'm about thirty, if my parents have anything to say about it. Brenda told my mom that you were all bandaged up like the Invisible Man. It looked like you'd gotten yourself into another accident."

"Did you tell her the truth?"

"Of course. But it didn't do any good. By that time, my parents were already deep into their Big Chill number."

"Maybe if they saw that being a daredevil has its good side," Judd mused. "Maybe if I did something heroic. Pulled a puppy off the tracks in front of a speeding train. Saved a boatload of drowning orphans."

"Judd," she said, grabbing him by the collar. "Don't you go risking life and limb just to prove a point to my parents."

"How else am I going to get to see you?"

"What?" Piper teased. "You don't count magic moments like this in the Hendersons' pantry?" She twirled, gesturing to the shelves of boxes and cans.

"Of course, my darling," Judd teased back, imitating a romantic lead in a corny old movie, "I live for these stolen minutes in the Cave of the Spaghetti-Os."

Then he took Piper completely by surprise by quickly kissing her in the middle of her laughter.

Tommy Henderson took them *both* completely by surprise by turning on the overhead light in the pantry and standing there in his Smurf pajamas, announcing, "Mom and Dad won't like it that you had your boyfriend here while you're baby-sitting."

"Go away, Tommy," Piper said.

"What if Connie or Bonnie got pneumonia or fell out a window while you were making out in here?"

"We were *not* making out," Piper said. "Judd just stopped by to lend me his geometry notes."

Tommy didn't even dignify this lie with a response. "They'll probably call *your* parents," he went on.

Suddenly Piper could see where this line of conversation was going.

"All right, you little blackmailer," she said. "How much?"

"Five dollars."

"*Outrageous!*" she shouted.

"Added to what you already owe me, that brings your account to twenty-eight dollars," he said, punching up the total on a little calculator he took from his pajama pocket.

"You owe *him* money?!" Judd said, incredulously, but laughing. It probably did look pretty funny. Tommy was only eight years old.

"It's really not funny at all," Piper said indignantly. "It's really quite a sad story. You'd better go, though — before he raises it to ten dollars."

Judd nodded and started out of the pantry. When he was at the door, he turned and asked, "What are we going to do about the twins? We have to make them pay. Does Tamara really have a plan?"

Piper nodded. "She does and you'll find out about it tomorrow."

"Until then, my dear," he said, back to impersonating the old-time movie star, covering his heart with his hand.

"Yes, Heathcliff. At our special place, our moor, our secret forest, our Casbah."

"Yes," he said, taking her hand and looking deep into her eyes. "Our homeroom."

Chapter 14

Piper hung out by her locker after school, putting her books away, taking them out again, putting them in again, trying some new lipstick, fooling around with her mascara — killing time until the twins came by on their way out. They finally did, walking together at their usual snail's pace, lost in their usual stream of gossip. Piper recognized straight away who they were talking about.

"T. Craig and Tiffany saw her riding in a limo with bulletproof glass," Cathy said, embellishing the story a little. "And that phony 'brother' of hers was driving. Isn't that proof positive she's . . ."

". . . a spy?" Casey finished the sentence. "Oh, yeah. That car's probably one of those spymobiles that throw out oil slicks and smoke bombs and stuff. It's time we put the word . . ."

". . . out on her," Cathy said. "For sure. She could be sneaking into the school offices. Gathering information for her files. It's practically our civic duty to warn the others against her."

Piper knew they could only be talking about Tamara. The twins had clearly gotten it into their heads that she was a foreign spy. Piper would have to stop them, before they really spread their stupid rumors. The last thing Tamara needed was to feel even more out of it around Fairwood High than she already did. But first, Piper had to settle *her* score with the "Tag Team of Trouble," as she thought of the twins.

"Oh, Casey and Cathy!" she called out, turning from her locker as they passed by. "Do you think you could do me a favor?"

"Uh . . ." said Casey.

"Well, actually . . ." said Cathy.

Always so helpful, Piper thought, but pressed on, knowing that when the twins heard what the "favor" was, they'd be overjoyed to do it.

"What I need is someone to pass a note to Judd for me. I'm pretty sure he's through with me. Actually, I think he has his eye on someone else. I don't know who, but I overheard him talking about someone, saying she was 'really fine.' So *I'm* really desperate. I want to give it one last try — to get him back. Could one of you possibly . . . ?" She pulled a folded note out of the pocket of her jean jacket.

"Let me!" Casey said, at the same time that her sister was leaping toward the note saying, "I'll do it!"

"Wow!" Piper said. "I can't ever remember you two being so helpful."

"Oh, we've turned over a new leaf," Casey said.

"Yeah," Cathy agreed. "We're helping old ladies across the street now, and helping at the hospital. But we've always got time to do a favor for a friend." And with that, she took the note from Piper's hand like a Venus's-flytrap snatching a fly out of midair.

Piper waited until the twins had disappeared around the corner of the hall, before closing her locker. Then she ran down to the girls' washroom, where Tamara was waiting for her.

"Phase One successfully completed," Piper said, brushing her hands together. "Tamara, you're a genius."

"Come then," Tamara said, but Piper had gotten distracted by the banks of mirrors and was giving her long blonde hair a quick brushing. Tamara watched her in the mirror and wondered if she, too, should get her ear pierced with three holes. The king and queen would probably not approve, though, she thought and sighed.

Piper heard the sigh and asked, looking at Tamara in the mirror, "Something wrong?"

"Just a royal matter," Tamara said and changed the subject. "Come on. If we don't hurry, we will miss the fun of watching the twins open that note."

"How are you so sure we'll be able to find them?" Piper wanted to know, as they walked to the school exit.

"Piper," Tamara said, pushing the school door open against the blustery wind. It was beginning to rain outside. "I'm surprised at your lack of perceptiveness. How can you think that for such an important moment the twins could be without — "

"Fries!" Piper said, guessing at once what Tamara was getting at.

Adolfo was waiting outside with an umbrella and for once, Tamara was glad to see him, and to get a fast ride in the Mercedes over to The Thermos.

"Boy," Piper said, whistling low. "Nice car." What she was thinking was that this must be the "bulletproof limo" the twins had been talking about. She had to stop their stupid gossip about Tamara. Piper was protective of her friend. Some of the time she even forgot that in her own country, Tamara was a princess. Here in Fairwood, she seemed more like an innocent newcomer who needed help in navigating the sometimes treacherous waters of Fairwood High.

Because it was raining so hard, most of the kids from school had just gone straight home. The Thermos was nearly deserted, and so they had no trouble spotting the twins, huddled in their favorite back booth. Casey was just shaking ketchup over the plate of fries between them. The note was still folded, on the table, a treat they were clearly savoring.

Piper and Tamara slid into the booth behind them and listened.

"The suspense is delicious, isn't it?" Cathy asked Casey. "Let's guess what she says in the note."

"Oh, Judd, darling!" Casey impersonated Piper. "*Please* don't leave me. Especially not for that *femme fatale* — Casey Connor. If you fall in love with her, I'll *never* get you back!"

"Of course, it really doesn't matter what she wrote, does it?" Cathy said. "*This* is the note Judd's going to think she wrote." She pulled a loose-leaf from her ring binder and read it over. "Do you think 'Dear Too Irresponsible' is too hostile an opening?"

"No," Casey said with delight. "It's perfect. But come on. I can't stand the suspense any longer. Let's see what snivelly, drippy things she said to him." And with that she picked Piper's note off the table and opened it. Her jaw slowly dropped open with surprise as she read aloud to her sister:

Roses are red.
Twins are two.
Noses should not
Be black and blue.
(But yours will be if we have to punch
them, which we will if you ever pull
another mean and stupid stunt like
this.)
> *Your homeroom pals,*
> *Piper and Tamara*
P.S. Learn to spell!

"But how did they . . ." Casey sputtered.
". . . find out?" Cathy finished the sputter.

In the next booth, Piper and Tamara covered each other's mouths with their hands to keep from giving their presence away with peals of laughter.

Chapter 15

"Do you think this is too many leaves?" Tamara shouted down from the top of the ladder. She'd been sticking red, yellow, and brown construction-paper leaves all over the walls in an attempt to turn a plain gym into a scene of the countryside in autumn.

Piper ran out to the center of the floor and gave her opinion.

"I don't think we can have too many leaves. I think our big problem is that we have too many pumpkins." She gestured toward the huge stack of them, which had been donated to the Fall Frolic decoration committee by T. Craig's father, who owned a small grocery chain in the area. The problem with his pumpkins was that each of them had stamped on it in sharp black letters, "T. Craig for President."

"Hey, you guys said you were going to

help *my* campaign," Tiffany wailed as she came through the door and saw the pumpkins.

"We *are*," Piper assured her, pointing to the big photos of Tiffany taped to the basketball backboards, but even as she said it, she knew two pictures were no match for a hundred pumpkins.

"Of course," Tamara said innocently from atop her ladder. "The decoration committee is grateful for all donations, but still, it is up to us to decide just how to display them to their best advantage. I myself think those pumpkins would be much more attractive if that lettering were turned to face the wall."

Tiffany and Piper had to laugh. Sometimes Tamara surprised them all with her ability to take action. But now it was Tamara's turn to be surprised as Coach Talbot stuck his head through the doorway.

"I took a few minutes off from practice to see how you girls were doing. If I'm going to have to chaperone a dance, I want it to be a good one. Oh-oh, looks like you've got a ways to go." He peered at the gym, which didn't look much different from the night before, when it had been the scene of a football pep rally.

"I think we need some help, Coach," Piper said. "The decoration committee is now about four hours behind schedule. At this rate, we ought to be done sometime tomorrow morning."

"But the dance is tonight!" Coach Talbot said.

"Precisely," Piper said.

"Okay, okay," the coach said. "I'll see if I can't rustle you girls up some helpers."

"*I'll* help," said Karen who had just turned up in the gym doorway. "I'll *try* to find the others, too."

"Don't bother looking for Judd," the coach said. "I've got him over at practice for the rest of the afternoon."

"And don't ask T. Craig," Tiffany said, drawing Karen aside. "We don't want him to see what we're doing to his advertising."

"I'll get Eddie, then," Karen said. "He won't *like* it, but he'll *do* it."

"Oh, good," Tamara said. "He is so artistic. He can arrange the scarecrow display."

"*Wait* a minute," Karen said. "Am I hearing *right*? Eddie Baker arrange any kind of display? Are we talking about the *same* Eddie Baker? Skinny guy? Sunglasses? Generally *surly* expression? The Eddie I know couldn't tell a paintbrush from a monkey wrench. All *he* does is hang out underneath his car."

Tamara came down off the ladder and said, thoughtfully, "This Eddie, I think, is a very complicated person. His looks, maybe they deceive."

Karen shook her head.

"This stuff is a *big* surprise to me. I went with him for *months* and *none* of what you're saying sounds like the guy I knew. But maybe I was always talking about my theater stuff so much *he* couldn't get a word in edgewise."

"What is this 'edgewise'?" Tamara asked.

"Oh, boy," Karen said, at a loss for a way to explain the concept. "I'll have to give that one some thought. In the meantime I'll go track down that grease monkey, and see if he'll give us a hand with these decorations. If we don't all pitch in, that gym, I'm afraid, is going to look exactly like a gym tonight."

As Tamara was watching Karen run off, she saw Coach Talbot.

"Coach," Tamara said, totally expecting him to listen to her. "There is something I am wanting to ask you. About American customs."

"Shoot," he said. "I don't know if I'll be able to answer your question, but I'll try."

"Is it proper for girls to ask boys to dance?" Tamara asked, now shyly.

"Around here, they usually have plenty

of 'ladies' choice' numbers. Just wait for one of them," Coach Talbot said.

"And is it also proper for students to ask teachers, or coaches, to dance?"

"Uh, well," said the coach, completely rattled by this question. "I'll have to look in my copy of the student handbook to see if that's covered." He smiled a nervous smile and turned to go. "Got to scare you girls up some reinforcements," he said as he ran off.

Tamara stood in the doorway for a few minutes reflecting on this exchange. On the one hand, the coach had not exactly jumped at the thought of dancing with her. On the other hand, he had not said no, or ruled out the possibility entirely. She decided to take this as a positive sign.

Three hours later, the gym was a different place. The expanded decoration committee stood and looked proudly at the setting they'd created for the Fall Frolic. With the rotating floodlights of yellow and orange playing across the leaves, and the giant slide projection of a fall forest behind the bandstand, the paper leaves, the turned-around pumpkins, the scarecrow standing under a gold paper moon, the hay-wagon refreshment stand — the gym had been successfully disguised as a fall scene.

"What time is it anyway?" an exhausted Piper asked the others.

Tamara looked at her gold watch. "Almost five-thirty."

"Yikes!" Piper said. "The dance starts at eight. My big night with Judd and here I am — totally grubby in my worst pair of paint-smeared khakis, my hair a tangled mess, and a zit on my chin."

"I, too, had better go home and change, or I will be un-ready for this festivity. I will especially be un-ready to dance with that chunk, Coach Talbot," Tamara said.

"Hunk," Piper corrected her. "Look, why don't we meet back here a little before seven. I want to give everything a last-minute check before the crowds show up."

"Why do I not pick you up on my way?" Tamara said.

"In the Princessmobile?" Piper asked, quietly so no one else would hear.

"Why not? All girls are princesses on the night of the dance, no?"

Chapter 16

Tamara slid deeper into her hot, hot bubble bath and laughed at the sound of Maria bustling about beyond the door, humming old Caprian folksongs from Tamara's childhood.

"You are happy tonight about something?" Tamara called out.

"Ah, yes," Maria said. "This is like at home. Getting you ready for a gala evening. I'm laying out your satin ball gown now."

"Oh no, Maria. This is a casual dance. Some of the students will just wear their jeans, Piper tells me."

"America," Maria sighed, opening the bathroom door and sticking her head in. "I cannot get used to its 'leisure look.'"

Tamara laughed and asked Maria to set out her pale green tweed skirt and white cotton sweater. Then she got out of her bath, dried off, and sprayed herself with her cologne. It was called Tamara, named after her by a Parisian perfumer.

She went over to the vanity and put on some light makeup. Because of her brilliant violet eyes and her flawless complexion, she used only the slightest hint of blush and a tiny bit of mascara. Her hair was her other great beauty asset. She took it out of its clip now, let it fall around her shoulders, and gave it a brushing. When she was done, she appraised herself in the mirror and thought she might be pretty enough to attract the notice of the very handsome football coach.

When she was dressed and ready, she ran back to the garage to find Adolfo. But he wasn't there. She ran up the stairs to his apartment and knocked on the door. She was answered by a low groan.

"Adolfo?"

Another groan. She turned the doorknob and let herself in. There, curled up on the sofa was a very pale and pained-looking Adolfo.

"I think I have gotten this 'bug' that is going around the school."

"The Twenty-Four-Hour Torture? You poor thing. I'll go and call a doctor," Tamara said, putting a hand on Adolfo's forehead.

"No," he said and groaned again weakly. "I am already better than I was. But I am thirsty."

"Then I will have Maria come up and bring you something to drink. And then you will rest while I drive myself to the dance."

"No! You shouldn't go alone!"

"Nonsense. It's just over to the school and back. And I won't be alone. I'm picking up Piper."

He tried to lift himself off the sofa pillows, but the effort was too much for him, and he dropped back against them again. Tamara decided to take his silence for consent and gently picked the car keys off the table, gave Adolfo's forehead a comforting pat, and left to get Maria.

Piper was so excited about the dance that she'd hopped off the living room chair and over to the window to look out a dozen times before she saw the blue Mercedes pull up. She was surprised to see Tamara get out from behind the wheel.

"I am your chauffeur for the evening. Adolfo has the bug, the poor boy," she explained to Piper at the door with a serious face. But then the traces of a smile began to form on her mouth as she said, "It looks like the only chaperone I'll have tonight is Coach Talbot."

"Tamara," Piper said as they backed down the driveway and pulled out onto the street. "Aren't you too young to drive?"

"Oh, no," Tamara replied. "I am sixteen, you know — older than you. And in Capria, I am a most expert driver."

"A few weeks ago I couldn't have predicted I'd be going to my first high school dance to see a secret boyfriend, chauffeured by a princess!" Piper said with disbelief.

"Yes, a lot of changes for both of us this fall," Tamara said. They were at the stoplight on Main and Palm. Tamara looked over at Piper. "You look very good in that outfit. Very mature."

"Thanks," Piper said shyly. "Black is my best color, I think. This is the outfit I was going to wear on my date with Judd. The date that never happened. I'm going to give it a second try tonight."

When they got to school, the gym was dark. They went to the switch box behind the bandstand, turned on the rotating colored lights, and turned the overheads to their dimmest setting.

"Perfect," Piper said, looking around at the scene.

"We did well," Tamara agreed. "I think I will make some changes in the ballrooms in the palace."

"This the Fairwood High gym? We in the right place?" asked the first of five guys dragging electronic equipment and musical instruments in cases through the doorway.

"You must be the band," Piper said.

"Yeah. We're The Shades." It was then that Piper noticed that all of them were wearing sunglasses. They were also stumbling into things. It was pretty dark in the gym now. She showed them to the bandstand and watched them trip up onto it, and hoped their music was better than their gimmick.

When she turned her attention back to the gym and looked for Tamara, she saw her talking to the twins! Piper went over, filled with suspicion. What were the bad sisters up to now?

"They have come to apologize," Tamara explained, and it was true that the twins did have sorry looks on their faces.

"We're . . ." Cathy said.

". . . sorry," Casey finished. "We really only meant it as a practical joke, but it went too far."

"You mean you're not after Judd?" Piper asked.

"Get real," Casey said, waving the suggestion away as if it was just ridiculous. "I've already got a boyfriend. He goes to Chopin. He's in their acting program, looks just like Michael J. Fox. We just wish he had a twin brother for Cathy."

Piper said, "I didn't know you were going with someone."

"Sure, he's coming later tonight so you'll probably get to meet him."

"But right now," Cathy said, "we have a surprise for you two."

"Yeah?" Piper said, looking around.

"No, not here," Cathy said.

"In the old gym," Casey said.

"But that is off-limits to students?" Tamara said. "I read that in the school paper. They are waiting to tear it down. It is very old and dangerous and we are not supposed to go in."

"Oh, the namby-pamby principal's office put that story out. They also gave that handout of safety tips that had all sorts of stupid stuff in it. Don't slam your fingers in your locker. Give me a break."

"Yeah," Cathy backed up her sister. "The old gym's fine. Kind of a neat place, really. Sometimes we go there just to hang out. It's so quiet and . . ."

" . . . private," Casey said.

"Anyway, Piper, Judd is there, waiting for you. He said we should bring you there."

Piper looked at the twins thoughtfully. "Why at the old gym? What is he doing there?"

Casey shrugged. "How should I know?

He just told me to get you there. I guess it seems romantic to him."

Piper hesitated.

Then Cathy laughed. "Okay, if you don't want to meet him, I'll be more than happy to."

"I didn't say I wasn't going," Piper said. She turned to Tamara and laughed. "It's really typical of Judd to do something like this. To want to meet me in a place we aren't supposed to be in."

Tamara looked at the twins and then said firmly to Piper, "I am going, too."

Piper gently pushed Tamara away. "Tamara, this is supposed to be a rendez-vous, not a homeroom meeting."

"You will just have to rendezvous with me, too," Tamara said. "I am not letting you go off alone with them." She moved her head in the twins' direction.

Piper sighed wearily and said, "Okay. I don't have time to argue with you."

They followed the twins down the dimly lit hallway leading to the far end of the school, where the old deserted gym was.

"Are you sure you want to do this?" Tamara asked Piper in a low voice, when they had been following the twins for a few minutes. "I don't want to get anyone angry with us, especially not the coach."

"Oh, I think it'll be okay. It's not as if

we're going to be hanging out in there all night. We're just going for a little while. Then we'll all go back to the dance," Piper whispered back.

"That is right," Tamara said, regaining her confidence in this venture.

"Here we are," Casey said, turning to Piper and Tamara as they stood in front of a rusty old metal door, marked with a forbidding sign:

DANGER!

DEMOLITION SITE — UNSAFE

KEEP OUT!

Casey pulled it slowly open. It screeched with lack of use.

"Are you sure you know your way around in here?" Piper asked nervously.

"Oh, *come on*, chicken," Cathy said, indicating that Piper should go in. "Judd is waiting."

"Yeah," Casey said. "You two go on in and we'll switch the lights on. We've figured out which switches still work in there."

"But . . ." Tamara said.

"What a couple of wimps," Casey said to Cathy, then turning to Tamara and Piper, she taunted, "Afraid of the big, bad gym?"

"Of course not!" Piper said, letting her pride win out over her better judgment for a moment. "Come on, Tamara."

Tamara nodded and followed Piper into the gym, which was pitch-black inside, like a cave.

"I can't see a thing, can you?" Piper asked, when they were inside.

"I think I don't like this," Tamara said in a very small voice.

"Hey!" Piper shouted. "Casey and Cathy. Can you turn those lights on in here?"

The only response she got to this request was the loud clanging of the gym door being shut.

"Hey!" Piper yelled. "What are you doing?" She felt her way toward the thin crack of light coming from under the closed door. Tamara followed her.

Before they could get to it, they both heard the sound familiar from so many mornings at the lockers. The sound of a padlock being snapped shut. Only this sound was louder. This lock was bigger. First Piper, then Tamara, then both of them together tried pushing against the door with all their might. But no matter how hard they pushed, it didn't budge.

"Judd," Piper shouted. There was silence.

"You know," Tamara said. "I do not think Judd is here. I think we have been grouped."

"Duped," Piper said. "And I think we have been, too. What a nerd I am."

"Twins?" Tamara yelled with a last shred of hope. "The door seems to be stuck. Could you please help us open it?"

From the other side of the metal door, they heard the pure glee of two bursts of overlapping giggles.

Piper turned to Tamara and said, "We're locked in here. And Casey will spend the night going after Judd."

The two of them stood absolutely still, absorbing the horror of their situation, and then at the same moment, both of them heard the same light, brushing sound coming from high in the old rafters. Piper didn't know what it could be. But Tamara, who had visited many times the famous Caves of Capria, knew this sound all too well.

In a low whisper, she told Piper, "Bats."

Chapter 17

Back at the dance, everyone was arriving, meeting their friends, checking out what everyone else was wearing. A few couples had started to dance.

T. Craig showed up in a tuxedo, all set to see his name in lights, or rather in pumpkins, and was furious when he saw what the girls had done.

"I don't think this is what my father had in mind when he donated these pumpkins," he told Karen and Tiffany stiffly.

"It was a unanimous decision of the decorating committee," Tiffany said, trying to hide her smile.

"You mean Tamara and Piper," he said gruffly. "Well, I see they decided it was just fine to put up those Mt. Rushmore-sized photos of *your* smiling face. I'd like to talk to those two — to register my complaint. Where are they, anyway?"

"Oh, I'm *sure* they're around *some-*

where," Karen said, scanning the gym. But she couldn't see them anywhere.

"Oh, come on, T. Craig. Lighten up," Tiffany said, giving him a knuckle rap on his arm. He looked at her closely, to see if she was making fun of him. Finally he let his guard down a little, and smiled.

"Oh, all right. I can take a joke as well as the next guy. I can be a sport," he said uncertainly.

"No hard feelings, then?" Tiffany said.

"No hard feelings." He looked around at the couples on the dance floor, rocked up and down a little nervously on the balls of his feet for a minute, then said, "Maybe you'd like to dance with me?"

"Oh, T. Craig," Tiffany said, her voice back to its usual, brisk tone, "I couldn't do that, now could I? People might take it the wrong way. They might imagine I'd come over to your side and given up the race."

"How could you even think such a thing?!" T. Craig said. But he said it so indignantly that Tiffany was sure she'd been right in guessing his hidden motives.

"Don't waste any more time talking to the competition, T. Craig," she advised him. "Get out there and mix it up with the voters! Boogie yourself some votes!"

He responded to this teasing by clearing his throat, flicking the ends of his bow tie, and looking past Tiffany as he set off toward the dance floor to ask Cathy Connor to dance.

It was a few minutes later that Karen felt a tap on her shoulder.

"Wanna dance?" a surly voice said.

She turned and looked at Eddie standing there in jeans and a white shirt, a diamond stud in his ear — *his* way of going formal. For a second, she felt all her old defenses go up again. She was, in fact, just about to say "No, thanks," when suddenly she remembered . . . dancing was the one thing they did great together, the dance floor was the one place they were a true team, a real couple.

Karen didn't even bother to say yes, or even to nod — just took his hand and walked out onto the dance floor. She turned and looked straight into his steady gaze as they began to move into the old familiar routines they'd practiced through long afternoons in her basement. Without a moment's hesitation, he fell into step with her, matching her moves, mirroring them. They were in perfect synch — two parts of the same dance machine.

Other couples moved toward the edge of the floor. Some stopped dancing entirely just to stand and watch as Karen and Eddie spun and whirled, crouched down to the ground, then leaped up toward the ceiling, shaking their bodies in ripples that ran from their shoulders down to their hips. Karen felt their eyes on her and Eddie, and for a brief moment, she felt like the star she wanted to be. She was exhilarated and couldn't help throwing her head back and letting out a wild peal of laughter, clapping her hands above her head, then snapping her fingers down by her sides. Eddie was laughing, too.

"We were great!" she said to him, as they collapsed onto each other when the music stopped.

"We were fabulous!" he agreed.

They stood that way for one long comfortable moment which suddenly, in a flash, turned intensely awkward. They parted nervously and neither could find a thing to say to the other. Where did they go from here? Finally Eddie broke the tension between them.

"Let's take a walk," he suggested. "Maybe we could talk a little."

She nodded and they walked off the dance floor and out of the gym.

Judd came in about the same time, searching the crowd for Piper. He couldn't see her anywhere, but assumed she was off doing some last-minute work on the decorations. He kept his eye on the doors, so he'd be sure to see her as soon as she came in. He wanted to have every possible minute of this night together — to make up for all the trouble they'd been through.

He was so focused on waiting for her that he didn't see anyone come up to him until he felt breathing next to his ear.

"Hi," came a husky voice. He just about jumped out of his high-tops.

"Oh, Casey," he said when he saw who it was. "Hi." He was being polite, but after what the twins had done to him and Piper, he wasn't up to being nice.

"Did Piper tell you how sorry my sister and I are about fooling with your notes?"

"No."

"Sometimes our little practical jokes weird people out. But we didn't mean any harm. Really. Anyway, I told Piper that already, but I wanted to tell you, too. We're really sorry," Casey repeated.

She sounded so sincere. Like she really meant it. What could he say? He looked around the gym restlessly. "Say, speaking of Piper, you haven't by any chance seen her tonight, have you?"

Casey bit her lip and looked as if she was trying to remember some minuscule detail.

"Uh, I think someone said she had a toothache. Had to go to the dentist on emergency. I think it was a wisdom tooth. Yeah, that was it."

"Wisdom tooth?" Judd said. "But I ran into Karen after practice and she said Piper had just gone home. That was less than an hour ago."

"I heard it was very sudden. A freaky tooth kind of thing," Casey said, then rushed on, "So what do you say, seeing as she's not here tonight, maybe you and I. . . ." Now that she had Judd with her, Casey became shy and couldn't look him in the eye. Instead she stared at the toes of her boots as she went on, "Maybe we could get to know each other better. Dance a little. Maybe stop at The Thermos afterwards. Have a little snack. You could give me a ride on your motor — "

She looked up to see how she was doing, how he was reacting to this, but what she saw, with a shock, was that she was talking to herself! Judd had disappeared. Quite a few other kids though, had gathered around to hear what she had to say in her one-sided conversation.

"What're you creeps looking at?!" she shouted at them. "I was just practicing some lines for this new movie I'm going to be in with Charlie Sheen."

"Oh, right, Casey."

"Yeah, sure."

The onlookers just made a little fun of her, then walked away. The twins already had a reputation around school for being liars.

Judd was high on the list of disbelievers. Which is why he had left Casey and rushed off through the crowd to try to find someone who might be able to tell him the real reason Piper wasn't there now. The tooth thing sounded phony to him.

Finally he found Tiffany. She'd be a reliable source — so responsible and serious. If anything, she was *over*-responsible and serious, sort of fifteen going on forty.

"Hi, Tiffany," he said. "Seen Piper?"

"Piper? I heard she had some tooth trouble. Tamara took her to some emergency dental clinic."

"Oh," he said. "Thanks." So, it really was true. He walked back across the room feeling like the unluckiest guy in the world. Here, finally, was his big night with Piper, and dentistry had to come between them. Then he felt selfish realizing that it was much worse for Piper, who was not only having no fun tonight, but was probably having a tooth pulled on top of it.

In his depressed state, he didn't even think to ask Tiffany where she had heard the news. If he had, he would have found out it was from Cathy Connor.

But, not knowing this, he was actually feeling guilty for having been so rude to Casey, and decided to apologize and ask her to dance to make amends. The Shades were just starting into an old four-four-beat slow song from the sixties. What Judd hadn't known was that this was the band's five-song medley of golden oldies, and that he was going to be locked in step with Casey for the next twenty minutes.

All the while her eyes were dreamily closed, his were wide open, still looking for Piper. In his fantasy, she would come to the dance in spite of just having her tooth pulled. She would walk through the door with her head tied up in a white bandage, like a cartoon character. Casey pulled back and saw Judd's face just as it was breaking into a smile at the thought of this. She took it as a smile of happiness on his part, that he was dancing with her.

I've done it! she thought. *I've stolen him him away from Piper Davids! She thinks she's so cool, so smart, but here I am dancing the night away in the arms of Judd Peterson, and there she is, cooling her heels in the old gym.*

Chapter 18

If they sat very still, Piper and Tamara could hear, far off in the distance, the thumping bass and squealing guitar riffs of the band. The reason they were sitting very still was so as not to rustle up the bats.

"What will we *do*?" Piper said in a low, despairing voice.

"Sorry," Tamara said. "My resources in situations like this are extremely limited. Being a princess, I know many things. How to greet foreign diplomats. I have met your President, and the Pope, and Tom Cruise, who once made a film in my country. I know how to conduct myself at coronation ceremonies, and how to wave at my subjects from my balcony. I can pour tea and launch a ship with a champagne bottle. But nothing in my training or background covers the situation of being locked in a bat-filled old gymnasium by devious twins."

"It *is* quite a mess we've gotten ourselves into, isn't it?" Piper said. "Maybe we ought to try to find another way out."

"Yes. My eyes are adjusting. I can make out rough shapes, can you?" Tamara asked.

"Mmmhmm."

"Let us try, then. Perhaps there is another door." Tamara thought for a moment. "Put your hands on my shoulders so that we stay together. I will lead. We will go along the wall, like mice feeling with their whiskers."

"Mice!" Piper yelled. "Eeek! I hadn't even thought of mice. What if there are mice in here, too?"

"Please Piper," Tamara said firmly. "Even if we are not feeling brave, we should try to *act* brave. Then maybe we will fool ourselves."

"Right," Piper said, but without much belief. She had never felt *less* brave in her life.

"We will also have confidence. There *will* be a back exit. It *will* be open."

They moved slowly.

"Oh my gosh!" Piper breathed out in fear as they stumbled into something huge. "It's some dead animal!"

"Piper," Tamara said in a stern tone of voice. "It is merely a gymnasium horse, for vaulting over."

"Oh," Piper said sheepishly. "Sorry for being such a wimp. Let's go on."

But no sooner had they gone a few more steps than Piper was yelling again. "Help! We're being trapped in a giant spider-web!"

Tamara got down on the floor to feel this and told Piper, "It is some old netting — from a tennis net. Volleyball maybe."

"Oh, of course. Silly me," Piper said.

"Perhaps you should sit here and wait for me to go and try the door." Tamara, trained for years to take command, to lead, was putting her parents' instructions into action.

"Oh, no," Piper said, putting a firmer grip than ever on Tamara's shoulders. "As soon as you leave, those little bats are going to come and pay me a visit, I just know it. No, for better or worse, I'm sticking with you."

Finally they found the back door. They reached a new low in their depression when they found that it, too, was shut tight, probably also locked from the outside.

Tamara said angrily, "When I get my hands on those terrible twins . . . !"

"No," Piper said. "You're too nice a person. You'll let them off too easily. Let *me* at them first."

They slumped down onto the floor, side

by side. Suddenly Piper thought she felt something brush against her cheek.

"Tamara! A bat! Let's get out of here!" She ran as fast as she could, tripping along the way over the many obstacles strewn around in the darkness, rushing past her friend on the way to . . . she didn't know where. She wasn't even thinking, just running. Until finally, she hit the door — the one that the twins had locked. She slammed her whole body against it, again and again, not even thinking of breaking the padlock, just irrationally trying to get out, a caged animal trying to break free.

Suddenly there was a new sound, not the rustling of the bats, not the slamming of girl against door. This was an eerie, slow creeeeeaking.

"Piper!" shouted Tamara from the middle of the room. "Run fast! Toward me! The vibrations — they're making the ceiling give way!"

Piper hesitated only an instant, then ran out of the way — just as the old rusted-out metal beam came crashing to the ground, along with a rush of ceiling plaster and concrete chunks. She found Tamara and the two girls clung to each other in a mixture of fright and relief.

"Are we alive?" Piper asked, only half joking.

"Yes," Tamara said, slowly making her

way over to the door. "But I think we are now not only *locked* in, but also *blocked* in." It was true. When Piper came closer, she could see that there was no longer even the thin crack of light coming from beneath the door. A wall of rubble had piled itself in front of it.

"Oh, what are we going to do now?!" Piper said, and began softly sobbing.

"Stop!" Tamara said, putting a hand over Piper's mouth. "Listen."

They both stood absolutely silent for a moment and soon Piper could hear what Tamara had. Voices. Growing louder. Two of them. A guy and a girl. They could hear them through a tiny air vent near the ceiling by the door.

"Help! Help!" the trapped girls shouted, climbing the pile of rubble to get closer to the vent. "We're in here!"

"Who is that?!" came the guy's voice.

"It's Piper . . ."

". . . and Tamara!"

"What are you two *doing* in there?" came the girl's voice. "It's Karen. I'm with Eddie."

"Oh, thank goodness you've found us!" Piper said. "The twins locked us in here!"

"Don't worry," Eddie said. "I'll just go get a hammer and bust this lock open."

"It will not do any good!" Tamara shouted. "A beam has fallen. The door is

146

blocked, and the other one seems to have been sealed off. We are trapped!"

"We'll go get Coach Talbot then," Karen said practically. *"He'll* know what to do."

"No. Please don't!" Tamara shouted back. "I don't want to get in trouble with him. It is forbidden to come in here. I don't want him to think I am a silly, immature girl — the kind who breaks the rules, and lets stupid twins trick her into such a trap as this!"

There was a long silence on both sides of the door as everyone tried to think of another way out.

Piper got the idea first. "Judd!" she shouted. "Go get Superboy!"

"Right!" Eddie said. "You've got it! Might as well put that daredevil to work. All he's been doing all night is moping around looking for you."

Somehow, even in the middle of this horrible dilemma, even with the plaster dust clouding around making them cough, even with the bats swooping through the rafters, as they had been ever since the crashing beam had disturbed them, even in the petrifying scary darkness of the old gym, Piper felt a small glow in her heart thinking that Judd had been missing her.

Chapter 19

Judd came down out of the high, shadowy reaches of the bleachers, where he'd been hiding from Casey Connor since managing to get away from her. At first it had just seemed like a friendly dance, but when Casey pressed her cheek to his, he tried to tell her he already liked someone else.

Casey had brushed this information away, as though it were too boring for words. "But Piper's not here tonight," she said, snuggling up to Judd. "And like they say, while the cat's away, the mice will play."

"Yeah," he'd said. "Well, this mouse has to go now. Catch you later, Casey."

Now he crushed his empty cider cup and tossed it in the leaf-covered trash basket, and stalked out of the dance. He'd been sitting in the bleachers thinking, and had figured out a way to call Piper's house and find out how she was.

He put a quarter in the hall pay phone and punched the buttons of her number. He crossed his fingers, hoping Piper herself would answer, or at least her sister Molly.

But, after three rings, it was a deep voice that said, "Hello?"

Her father.

Judd quickly pinched his nose between his fingers, and said in the extremely nerdy voice that came out, "Is Piper Davids there?"

"No, I'm sorry, she's not."

Was she still at the dental clinic? He imagined her in the chair, a dentist with huge pliers hovering over her. Poor Piper!

"Do you know when she *will* be?" he said in this nerd voice.

"Who *is* this?"

"Uh . . . this is Roy Smith. I'm her lab partner in biology. I just wanted to let her know I got the frogs for our project."

"Frogs?"

"Yes, could you leave that message, please? When she gets home from the dentist?"

"What dentist? She's at the school dance."

"She's at the *dance*?!" Judd shouted, forgetting to pinch his nose, sounding exactly like himself, not caring, not bothering to say good-bye before he hung up and ran back into the gym. "I've got to find those twins!" he said to himself as he ran.

It wasn't too difficult. Casey was standing about two inches from where he'd left her, talking with her sister.

"You want to dance some more, Judd?" she said, not seeing the fury on his face.

"No, Casey. I do *not* want to dance. I want answers. Where is Piper? And Tamara? I can't find her, either. I know they were planning to come to the dance together."

Casey inspected her nail polish. "Maybe they decided to do something else."

"Yeah, maybe they went bowling instead," Cathy added, giggling.

Judd turned on his heel and stomped out of the gym. There was no point in talking to the twins, who would only give him doubletalk in return. He had a feeling they knew more than they were telling, and probably had something to do with Piper and Tamara's disappearance, but he'd never get it out of them. He'd have to find the girls on his own.

First, he ran out to the parking lot. There in the far row was Tamara's blue Mercedes. They were here someplace. But where? He ran back into the school. Tiffany and T. Craig were talking with a small group of serious-looking kids. Probably discussing issues with their potential voters. Some kind of impromptu mini-debate. Did those two ever just relax and have a good time?

"Hey," he said, pulling them both away. "Come and help me. Here's a real issue for you to sink your teeth into — Piper and Tamara are missing!"

"You mean they're not at the dentist?" Tiffany said innocently.

"Just where did you hear that, anyway?"

For a second she couldn't remember, but finally she said, "I think it was Cathy Connor."

"Aha!" Judd said. Now he knew he was on the right track. But which way did it lead? He turned to the other two. "All I know is they're here somewhere in the school. Will you help me look for them?"

"Sure," T. Craig said.

Tiffany nodded, then asked, "But where do we even start? This is a pretty big place, what with the new school, and what's left of the old buildings they're going to tear down."

It was as if a light went on inside Judd's mind.

"I'll bet that's it! The old buildings!"

They went through the double doors at the far end of the 400 wing, into the old school.

They decided to check every one of the abandoned classrooms and broom closets and stairwells. They had barely started, though, when they spotted Karen and Eddie running toward them from the darkened end of the old corridor.

"You guys!" they both shouted, then stopped, out of breath.

"Piper and Tamara . . . *trapped* . . . old gym!" Karen said in gasping bursts as she tried to catch her breath.

"Twins," Eddie gasped.

Judd looked around at the others. "What are we waiting for?! Let's go!"

When they got to the locked door, Judd shouted toward the vent, "Piper!"

"Judd? Is that you?"

"Yeah. I've brought the others. We're going to get you two out — somehow. Just hang in there."

He grabbed the padlock and asked Karen and Eddie, "Do the twins have the key? Is this their dirty work?"

"Yes, but it's no use getting the *key*," Karen said. "Something happened in there. Part of the *ceiling* fell in. A beam, too. The door's *completely* blocked."

"There must be another door," Judd said.

"They checked," Eddie said. "It's sealed. And they don't want us to tell the teachers or the coach. They're afraid they'll get in trouble for being in there in the first place."

"Then," Judd said, thinking about the problem, "we'll have to get creative."

He shouted through the vent, "Piper. Tamara. Are there any high windows, a skylight maybe? Any way you can see for me to get in?"

"There is a skylight," Tamara's voice came through the vent. "But it is where the bats gather."

"Bats!" Everyone outside said at once. Judd's face took on an expression of intense concentration. When he spoke, it was to get everyone into action.

First he shouted toward the vent. "You two, get into a corner *away* from that skylight. I'm coming through.

"Eddie and T. Craig, come with me and help me find the equipment I'll need. Karen and Tiffany, you go around outside the gym and scope out the easiest way I can get up the side of it. We'll all meet back here in five minutes."

By looking in three or four janitor's closets as well as the old basement, the guys were able to come up with a lot of old rope, a flashlight and a couple of grappling hooks and pulleys.

"Not optimum equipment," Judd said,

inspecting it, "but it ought to work in a pinch. And this is a pinch if I ever saw one."

The girls led them around the back of the old gym.

"Here," Tiffany said, pointing to a wall that went up two stories to a small roof, and then to the top of the building. "If you go this way, you can take the climb in two stages."

"You'd make a good mountain guide, Tiffany," Judd said, as he looped one of the ropes through the eye at the end of the grappling hook.

After knotting it, he gave it a tug to make sure it was secure, looked at the others and said, "Well, here goes nothing, as they say." And with that, he heaved the hook and pulley upward. A perfect toss. It snagged over the edge of the first roof. Judd rubbed his hands together, tied one end of the rope around his waist, grabbed onto the other, and began pulling himself along as he walked up the side of the old building. The others held their breath as they watched his feet groping for footing each time he swung back toward the wall.

"Way to go!" Eddie yelled out by way of encouragement.

"Hang in there, Superboy!" T. Craig

said, but this time there was no sarcasm in his voice.

"Yeah," Karen shouted. "You're doing *fine!*"

But she spoke just a little too soon. Suddenly Judd tried to boost himself on a jutting brick, but just as he thought he had a foothold, the brick crumbled and gave way beneath him. He hung there, midway up the two-story face of the old building, rubbing his ankle.

"You okay?" Eddie shouted.

"Not sure," Judd admitted. "Hurt my ankle, I think. I can probably still make it, though."

"Hang on, Judd!" Karen shouted. "*I'm coming!*"

"You?!" T. Craig said, looking at her with amazement. "But girls — "

"Yeah, T. Craig . . . ?" Karen said, staring him down. "Girls what? Girls don't get to scale buildings? Well, I'll tell you, if all my years in dance and gymnastic classes haven't got me in shape enough to scale that little old gym, I've been wasting a lot of time." She turned to Eddie. "Help me with that rope, will you?"

"We're not going to let her do this, are we?" T. Craig asked Eddie.

Eddie said, "If she says she can do it, she can do it."

Karen smiled and gave Eddie's ear an affectionate tug.

"And T. Craig," Tiffany added for good measure, "I hope you're not planning to get the feminist vote with that attitude."

Karen wasn't paying attention to any of this. She'd already taken several tries and finally managed to throw her hook onto the roof. She started up the building, toward Judd, who was still dangling in mid-air.

When she got to him, she told him, "Stay a little behind me. When I make contact with the side of the building, you can grab onto me to give yourself a boost. That way you won't have to use your ankle so much."

"Are you strong enough to take my weight?" he asked.

She nodded. "Let's give it a try."

It worked. He followed her all the way up. They made it onto the first roof and sat down to look at his ankle.

"I think I just sprained it a little," he said. "Luckily Ms. Creedy's first aid class isn't anywhere in sight. I ought to be all right. But I don't know if I can do much more wall scaling."

"Look!" Karen said. "We're in luck!" She was pointing to a metal ladder running up the side of the building to the top roof. "Can you handle that?"

"Piece of cake," Judd said. "Let's go!"

Within minutes they were on top of the second roof.

"Quite a view from up here," Karen said, looking around. "How's your ankle holding out?"

"I think I'll live," Judd said, then looked over Karen's shoulder. "Look. There's the skylight. Now comes the scary part."

Karen nodded, knowing what was coming. "I'm with you. Let's *go* for it."

They both found bricks, hesitated only a second in fear, then simultaneously heaved them through the sooty glass of the old skylight. In rapid sequence there was, first, a huge shattering of glass and, then, the rush of a dozen small black bats soaring and flapping through the opening. Karen and Judd held their arms protectively over their heads and watched the bats silhouetted against the fall moon as they shot into the night sky.

"Wow!" they both said, and then laughed with relief.

Once they'd cleared a space big enough in the glass, they lowered their bodies through it, and found themselves on a catwalk above the gym floor.

"Piper! Tamara!" Judd shouted. "We're here. Karen and I."

"Judd!" Piper said.

"Karen?" Piper and Tamara said in unison.

"We weren't expecting you to drop in like this," Piper joked.

Meanwhile, with their flashlight, Karen and Judd found an easy place to jump from the catwalk onto the gym's balcony, and from there took the stairs down onto the floor, where they found themselves hugged by a grateful Piper and Tamara.

"Our hero!" Piper said, giving Judd a fat kiss.

"And heroine!" both she and Tamara added, giving Karen a hug.

"Are you going to take us back out now?" Piper asked.

"We can't go back the way we came in," Judd said, rubbing his ankle. "I barely made it myself — wouldn't have without Karen's help. It's too risky. We have to find another way."

"I think I've got it," said Piper, who had taken the flashlight and was prying a grate off the wall. "I stumbled against this in the dark and suspected it was an air shaft. Look, it's big enough for us to crawl out through."

"Yes," Tamara said, "but where does it lead?"

"We'll soon find out," Piper said, signaling the others to follow her.

The tunnel wound around and around. It

was dark and extremely dusty. The four of them crawled single file, each secretly hoping they wouldn't run into any nasty surprises along the way.

After what seemed like a long, long time of crawling, they began to hear something. Music. Louder and louder. And then they were at another grate, beyond which they saw shifting colors of light.

"Could it be?" Piper said.

"I think it just might be," Judd said, as the four of them pushed against the grate and all tumbled at once out onto the floor of the new gym — right in the middle of a hundred couples dancing the last dance of the Fall Frolic.

Chapter 20

The four adventurers looked a sight — covered with soot and plaster, and dust and dust balls, their clothes torn, Judd limping to favor his sprained ankle. The whole gym full of kids stopped to stare in surprise at these grinning wrecks. And then the crowd parted to let Coach Talbot through.

"I'm sure you all have a perfectly reasonable explanation. Taking a shortcut back from the cookies and punch table in the cafeteria, no doubt." He was being sarcastic, but there wasn't any meanness to his words.

Judd, Piper, and Karen talked at the same time, their words overlapping, to recount what had happened. Only Tamara remained silent. She was embarrassed at having gotten herself into such a foolish scrape, doubly embarrassed for having to appear so foolish in front of Coach Talbot.

160

Especially a Coach Talbot all dressed up in his handsome chaperoning clothes — navy blazer and crisp khakis.

Tamara couldn't resist moaning, "The worst thing about this is that I missed my chance to ask you for a ladies' choice dance."

The coach blushed more than usual and said, "Well, maybe it's just as well. Jolene is turning out to be a pretty jealous fiancée." As he said this, he reached over and took the hand of — Ms. Finster!

Tamara stood there not knowing whether to laugh or cry. Cry at the news that the coach was going to marry someone else. Or laugh at the image Tamara couldn't suppress — the lifetime of Sloppy Joes poor Coach Talbot had ahead of him.

Judd took Piper's hand and said, "If I could walk enough to dance, I'd ask you for this last one. Some date, eh? Do you think we're ever going to *have* a date?"

"Oh," Piper said, smiling, "I think when my parents hear how Superboy rescued this particular damsel in distress, we'll be able to have all the dates we want."

"Superboy and Super*girl*," Judd reminded her, putting an arm around Karen. "She's really the one who saved the day."

By this time, Eddie and Tiffany and T.

Craig had arrived on the scene and Eddie congratulated Karen in his own way — with sarcasm.

"We all knew you were climbing your way to success," he teased, "but this is ridiculous."

T. Craig came up to Tamara and said, "What I don't understand is why, if you're a spy, you didn't just use your infrared scope to find a way out."

"Spy?" Tamara said, "Who has been saying this?"

"I'll give you two guesses," Piper said, "and that's how many it'll take."

"Those twins!" Tamara said. "Doing all these dirty tricks, and now spreading lies about me."

"But if you're not a spy, why do you have that guy lurking about all the time, and a limo and no parents around and all that?" T. Craig forged on in his deliberate way.

Tamara looked concerned. Then she said firmly, "I have my reasons."

"Oh, brother," Eddie said.

"What has your brother to do with this?" Tamara asked.

Everyone groaned.

I'll tell them soon, Tamara thought. But not quite yet.

"What are we going to do about Double

Trouble, anyway?" Piper asked, changing the subject quickly. "I see they've conveniently disappeared for the moment. But if they think that means they're off the hook. . . ."

"What about a week of Homeroom Hell?" Karen suggested. "You know — sand in their gym shoes, onions in their lockers, gum on their desk seats."

"Too light a sentence," Tamara said.

"I've got an idea," Tiffany said mysteriously. She smiled and said, "I'll tell you all Monday — in homeroom."

Chapter 21

Monday morning in 434, Coach Talbot was late and the atmosphere was close to total pandemonium. Everyone wanted to talk about all that had happened Friday night. Well, almost everyone. The twins sat, unusually silent, at desks in the farthest back corner of the room. Even rarer, they appeared to be completely absorbed in their schoolbooks.

When Eddie came in, he went straight over to Karen and said, "How you doing? No serious bruises or anything?"

She shook her head. "No, I'm fine." She was surprised at his concern.

"You were really impressive, you know," Eddie went on. "Seeing you scale that wall, without any concern for yourself, just to help someone in trouble, well . . . it kind of gave me a new take on you. I thought to myself, maybe Karen's finally growing up. About time, too."

Karen narrowed her eyes and fixed Eddie with a hard stare.

"*You* never change. *That's* what you thought, eh? Well, thank you so much. I'll be sure to use you as a reference if anyone ever wants to check on my maturity."

"You do that," Eddie said. Then he softened a little. "Look, this is going all wrong. I was trying to lead into talking about us at least being friends."

"You ... and me?" Karen said, as though she couldn't have heard him right.

"Yeah. Why not?"

"Well, for *one* thing, I'm going to be *extremely* busy for the next few weeks. *Both* newspapers called to interview me, and one of the teen magazines wants to do a mini-profile. I think all of this could be the start of something *big*, as they say. So you see, I really need to focus on my *career* for now. I can't. . . ." She didn't have a chance to finish her sentence. Eddie was already across the room, slumped into his desk, pulling a paperback out of his knapsack. Ignoring her with a vengeance.

Meanwhile Piper was breaking *her* bad news to Judd. "My parents saw the whole thing in the paper," she told him.

"Let me guess," he said, beaming. "They think I'm a big hero. They want me to be your steady guy. They want to take me on vacation to Hawaii. Buy me a Jaguar when I turn sixteen."

"Close," she said. "They say now they're *really* convinced you're a madman. I'm forbidden to see you again until you're at least fifty years old."

"Fifty?"

"They think maybe by then you'll have calmed down a little," Piper said, sadly.

"This can't be true, Piper! I thought they'd change their minds about me."

"Well, they didn't," Piper groaned. "You can't come over to my house. I'm not allowed to go to yours. Tommy Henderson will double my blackmail if you show up there again. I'm afraid all we have left, the only place we can see each other is — "

"Wait!" he said, holding up his hand. "Don't tell me. *Homeroom!*"

They both laughed sadly, in spite of what they felt was the true tragedy of the situation.

Piper looked around the strange and really ridiculous room. "I can't believe the only place we'll be able to see each other is *here* . . . in this ugly room. What a place for a romance."

Judd took Piper's hand and held it. "Your parents have to change their minds. I'll think of some way to make them know the real me."

Piper felt nervous suddenly . . . very

nervous. "Judd, leave well enough alone. At least, they haven't had me pulled out of homeroom. Don't do anything drastic. Things will work out . . . somehow . . . maybe . . . I think. Although my parents can *really* be stubborn."

As they were talking, Tamara came in, extremely agitated. "Adolfo is so upset!" she told them. "He came out of his flu on Saturday morning and saw the newspapers. He guards me for weeks and the one night he's sick, I get locked into a gymnasium and rescued through an air shaft. He was sure he would be dismissed from the Royal Union of Bodyguards. Finally Maria and Tomás and I assured him we would not let anyone in Capria find out."

"So why are you still upset if it's all straightened out?" Piper wondered.

"Because now he says he is *never* going to let me out of his sight! He will be my shadow. I will have no chance for a normal American teenage social life."

"Oh, I don't know," Judd said. "I think most of the kids are getting used to him hanging around."

"Maybe if we could get him some more casual clothes." Piper mused.

"A sweatshirt and jeans?" Tamara said with a smile.

"Yes!" Piper said. "Just the thing!"

"We will take him to the mall!" Tamara

said, laughing, but suddenly the laugh died on her face. She had spotted the twins, pretending to be deep into studying in the back of the room.

"What are we going to do about those wicked sisters?" Tamara asked. Tiffany, who'd been sitting on the coach's desk, talking with T. Craig, overheard, and clapped her hands for silence in the classroom.

"Before the coach gets here, we have some homeroom business to attend to. The matter at hand is, what can be done with a pair of extremely rotten twins?"

"Just a minute. I object to that!" Casey shouted.

"*Be quiet*," Tiffany said. "I have the floor. Parliamentary procedure. As I was saying, what does a homeroom do when two of its members play an incredibly dirty trick on two other members?"

"It was only . . . " Casey started.

". . . a joke," Cathy finished.

"Don't insult us with that nonsense," said Tiffany, who was in total command of the situation. "We all know you're the ones who locked Piper and Tamara in the gym. Either you accept our penalty, or else."

"Or else what?!" Cathy demanded, full of false bravado.

Tiffany just coldly stared her down and repeated in menacing tones, "Or *else*."

"Okay, okay," Casey said. "We'll go along with your little stunt. Just to show we're good sports. So — what is it you've got in mind?"

"We're giving you both a mandatory assignment at the Halloween Fun Fair, of which I just happen to be chairperson."

"You have a particularly nasty assignment in mind I hope?" Piper asked.

"I was thinking of the Pie Witches," Tiffany said.

"Pie Witches?" Eddie said, curiosity pulling him out of his sulk.

"Yes, the twins will get to dress like the little witches they are and sit on a shelf while people pay to throw cream pies at them."

"All right!" everyone said, approving of Tiffany's punishment, as the twins grumbled to each other.

"Pies will be their *just desserts*," Judd added, and everyone groaned at his terrible pun. Except for Tamara, who didn't get the joke, and beyond that had a more basic question.

"What is this *Halloween*?" she said.

The homeroom group looked at her, then at each other, laughed, and all together, began to try to explain.

When they quieted down, Piper looked around the room. "What a group we are. Judd and I can only see each other in homeroom. Karen and Eddie barely speak. T. Craig and Tiffany are so competitive, they make the Superbowl look like amateur night. The twins are abominable and you *know* are going to cause more trouble. I don't believe us. And all I see ahead are more problems."

"It's *drama*," Karen said.

"It stinks," Eddie argued.

"It's a challenge," Judd announced.

"What is this 'stinks'?" Tamara asked.

"You'll find out," Tiffany said. "Probably sooner than you want."

What happens when Tamara tries acting like a typical American teenager, and falls for the *most* unlikely guy in homeroom 434? Read Homeroom #2, *The Princess of Fairwood High*.